WINGS OF THE PIRATE

Look for other Western & Adventure novels by
Eric H. Heisner

Africa Tusk

Conch Republic, Island Stepping with Hemingway

Along to Presidio

West to Bravo

Seven Fingers a' Brazos

T. H. Elkman

Short Western Tales: Friend of the Devil

Follow book releases and film productions at:
www.leandogproductions.com

WINGS OF THE PIRATE

Eric H. Heisner

Illustrations by Al P. Bringas

Visit our website at
www.leandogproductions.com

Illustrations by: Al P. Bringas
Contact: al_bringas@yahoo.com

Dustcover jacket design: Dreamscape Cover Designs
Based on 1st Edition cover design by: Clint A. Beach

Paperback ISBN: 978-0-9995602-9-7
Second Edition

Printed in the United States of America

Dedication

To my children who inspire art,
and my wife who inspires the rest.

Special Thanks

Tim Haughian, Al P. Bringas, Amber W. Heisner,
Gena Kay, Ryan Pemberton, Pemberton & Sons Aviation

Introduction

The guttural roar of a radial engine and the whirl of spinning props in the air or on terra firma from a WWII aircraft is something that vibrates and thunders through your soul. As a child, my first airshow was a thing of wonder and amazement. I was permanently hooked on vintage aviation—flying boats in particular— when I was lucky to witness the Spruce Goose, the colossal air-ship that dreams are made of.

From that impressionable young age forward, adventure for me has always been old west cowboys and seaplanes! I have been fortunate to have my Western novels published and distributed worldwide, including *West to Bravo* and *T. H. Elkman*. Now it is time to stretch my literary wings to explore my other passion of naval aviation and water-flying.

Wings of the Pirate is an old-fashioned adventure tale I have fantasized about since my time in elementary school. Back then, I was sketching pirate treasure on journals and doing mock water landings with everything that could make a wing inside that wooden classroom desk. Reel your mind back to those days of youthful imagination and exploration while enjoying an exciting journey into the South Pacific...

Eric H. Heisner

January 9, 2017

WINGS OF THE PIRATE

In the years immediately following the second Great War, the influence of the western world hung heavy on the islands of the South Pacific. The harvest of new economic resources provided a wealth of prosperity to those who could afford the gamble. While most rushed to invest in the new-found abundance, others merely planned to steal it. . .

Chapter 1

Moving across the wide expanse of ocean, a large sailing yacht gleams in the clear, sunlit day. The sharp wooden hull cuts through the surface and cascades water into the wake. The indigo waters of the South Pacific roll with small caps of white that occasionally lick up toward the vast blue of sky. Alone, the vessel makes a picturesque figure on the seemingly endless canvas of aquatic seascape.

Two scantily-clad women sunbathe on chaise lounge chairs on the foredeck of the ship. Their bodies glisten with tanning-oil and sweat, as the afternoon sun bakes them to a golden hue of bronze. Coming down the stairs from the wheelhouse, a shirtless man strolls toward the two women and talks with them momentarily. He gives each of them a friendly kiss and moves away, disappearing below deck.

~*~

Somewhere on the broad, empty horizon, the low rumbling roar of engines is heard echoing in the distance. Turning over to their backs, the two sunbathers reach out to put on over-sized sunshades. They pull back their hair and position skimpy suit tops to conceal a small portion of their exposed figures from the ever-present yacht crew.

The distinct humming vibration of multiple airplanes grows closer. With curiosity, the women sit up, clutch their bikini tops, and scan the surrounding blue waters. Approaching from the western horizon like phantasms in the afternoon sun, two Consolidated PBY Catalina seaplanes hover fifty feet above the water.

Crewmen in the top rigging of the yacht temporarily stop their tasks to observe, and the pair of sunbathers wave as the matte-black military warplanes thunder past overhead. Flying several ship-lengths beyond the designer yacht, the two seaplanes tip their wings, bank against the horizon, and circle back toward the sailing ship. Slowly dropping from the sky, the hulls of the air-ships dip into the ocean waters and glide on the step like winged speedboats.

As the flying warbirds become more boat than aircraft, the sleek frames sink lower into the water and plough forward. The ocean swells splash over the forward-facing machine gun turrets and catch the spinning orange tips of the radial-powered propellers. Glistening, like lethal black cats low on the prowl, the two warplanes creep toward the cruising yacht.

The owner of the sailing vessel steps from below with a white linen shirt draped across his tan shoulders.

He walks to the starboard rail and watches the Catalina seaplanes taxi toward him. Turning to the wheelhouse, the man signals the engineer to idle the engines and cut the sails. The yacht's big diesel engines drown to an idle and the crew pulls up canvas in the rigging. The man watches, as the nose hatch on one of the seaplanes is pushed open to reveal a dark cavity beneath.

The leading seaplane slowly taxies closer to the yacht. From the front hatch emerges a sleek, tan-skinned man in an ivory-colored suit, gray fedora, and with a dark leather eye-patch. He gives a curt wave, which is returned by the owner of the yacht, while the seaplane moves within several feet of the glossy wooden hull of the sailing ship.

Air Captain, P. M. Rasmus has a full head of stippled gray hair to show for his chronologically enhanced years. Appearing to be in prime physical condition for his age, his serious demeanor shows through his refined body language. His lone, piercing steel-blue eye scans the yacht's features and observes as the other PBY seaplane moves around to the portside of the sailing ship.

From the foredeck of the yacht, a crewman rolls down a rope ladder that swings outward from the cantilevered hull. At the nose hatch, Captain Rasmus reaches out and takes a firm grip on the wooden rung. With the agility of a lifelong sailor, Rasmus nimbly steps from the seaplane and climbs the swaying rope ladder to the deck rail.

Followed by two of his crewmen in surplus military flight gear, Rasmus steps over onto the deck.

His eye twinkles with interest as the lone orb gazes over the forecastle. He is met by the yacht's owner, buttoning his linen shirt, and the pair of women, beside him, in skimpy sunbathing outfits. The attentive women snicker between themselves, as they curiously look him over. The yacht proprietor steps forward and offers his hand. "Welcome. Who do I have the honor of bringing aboard?"

Captain Rasmus declines the shake of the man's hand and tips his gray felt fedora while bending to offer a half bow.

"Greetings. . . My name is Captain P. M. Rasmus. How are you good folks this fine afternoon?"

One of the women jiggles excitedly in her two-piece bathing suit and flashes Rasmus a toothy grin. "Oooh, aren't you the dashing one!"

A sly smile creeps across Rasmus' stone features.

"Thank you, ma'am. I try to be civil."

Behind the captain, the airmen silently watch the crew's movements and assess the ocean craft's layout. Rasmus remains rigid, and his cold, direct manner starts to infuse an element of tension into the encounter. The yacht-owner makes an attempt at being the courteous host and motions over a crewman, who rolls up the liquor cart. He lifts an already poured cocktail from the lavish setting and gives a sweeping wave in offering. "Would you and your crew like a drink?"

Rasmus turns a steely gaze toward the man, and the hint of a grin drops from his features. "No, I'm quite sorry. You see, we still have a lot of work to accomplish."

With a swirl of his cocktail, the man takes a long sip and looks at Rasmus over the rim of the short glass.

"Oh, where are you headed?"

The almost clear, blue eye of Captain Rasmus sharply scans the ship's deck and calculates the positions of nearly all the members aboard. "Nowhere in particular... Wherever our work leads us."

One of the women leans her generous bosom over the lacquered wood railing and smiles down at the dark-painted PBY Catalina seaplane still idling below. She stares curiously at the side of the flying boat, which is adorned with a small emblem of a winged skull positioned over a three-bladed airplane propeller. The woman adjusts herself from nearly falling out and giggles toward the Air Captain.

"How exciting! What do you do flying around with your big, black, floating airplanes?"

Rasmus turns and forces an uncomfortable smile.

"They are boat-planes. Seaplanes, if you prefer."

The ice clinks against the glass of his mixed drink as the yacht-owner peers over the railing. He notices a large-caliber machine gun turret at the nose and one at each observation blister of the water-flying craft.

"What do you do exactly?"

"We are Air Pirates."

Catching the man mid-swallow on his cocktail, Rasmus watches coldly as the surprised fellow chokes and laughs through his nose. Finally putting his drink aside, the yacht-owner smiles, amused at Rasmus. "That's pretty funny, with the eye-patch 'n all. What do you do, seriously?"

The two women stare at the one-eyed, humorless air-captain strangely, not knowing exactly how to interpret him. Two of Rasmus's air crew step forward and produce automatic pistols from concealed holsters in their flight suits.

Captain Rasmus stares icily at the yacht owner and his two companions. "Oh, sir, we are quite serious."

Rasmus nods slightly to the air-pirate positioned on his right, and the man points his already-cocked pistol skyward. The sharp crack of the gunshot sends a chilling message and stops everyone short, as a whiff of burned gunpowder floats in the breeze. Immediately following, the only sound is the small *tink* of the brass shell-casing, as it bounces on the ship's wooden deck.

Chapter 2

In a burst of movement, the rest of the air pirates scurry from the hatch of the idling seaplane onto the waiting rope ladder. Before anyone can take a breath, pirates swarm over the railing and, with weapons at the ready, occupy the foredeck. The yacht owner and two women gape in amazement at the military-like operations of the boarding party.

A crewman watches over the sailing vessel's port-side rails as the nose-hatch pops open on the other seaplane and pirates spill out with machine guns and grappling hooks. They spread out across the high wing and coordinate their movements in a well-practiced maneuver. The roped hooks are thrown onto the yacht and hold fast as the pirates advance on the vessel.

In less than a minute, the deck of the yacht is teeming with gun-toting air pirates. The dubious crew of buccaneers appears to be a mix of international, former military, paid mercenaries with war surplus outfits and the ingrained knowledge of discipline, firearm handling, and fierce combat. With pistols and machine guns locked and loaded, they line up the well-dressed civilian boat crew along the foredeck.

Like a coach running drills, Captain Rasmus observes the precision of his men. His cold, steady gaze studies every movement on the captured civilian yacht. An arm crosses his chest to rest on the other as he stands in resolute command. He licks the hint of salt air from his lips and touches under his eye, satisfied, as the yacht crew is assembled on deck before him. "Now, if everyone could please make their way to the bow, we won't have any problems."

The owner of the yacht stares dumbfounded at the quickly escalated situation and turns to the air pirate leader. He takes a step toward Rasmus and raises his voice. "What the hell is this? You can't be serious!"

In one fluid motion, Rasmus reaches into his suit jacket, slides out a Luger pistol and presses it to the man's forehead. "Really?" Rasmus holds the gun firm and narrows his eye. "How serious do you think I am?"

Silently staring at the pistol pushed high on his brow, the yacht owner feels the cold chill of reality sweep over him. Sweat beads on the man's temples as he fights the urge to shrink away.

Rasmus remains quiet for a moment, then turns to address the crew. "Now that everyone is serious..."

The explosive discharge of a shotgun turns everyone's attention to the walkway on the upper ship deck. A pirate tumbles backward down the stairway and lays in a bloody mess at the bottom. With the exception of the big diesel engines below deck, still at an idle, there is complete stillness. A tense silence ensues as everyone stares at the blood-spattered body, nearly cut in half at the foot of the stairs.

The sailing ship slowly rises and falls on the ocean swells and nobody speaks. A flush of anger explodes from Rasmus, and he spits his words like venom. "Bring me whoever did that!"

With the Lugar still held to the forehead of the owner, Rasmus turns to him, swallowing hard to regain his calm demeanor. "Oooh, bad timing. Bang!!" With a quick jab, Rasmus forcibly shoves the man's head away with the business-end of the aimed pistol.

The yacht owner stumbles backward and touches the round marking on his forehead left by the barrel of the gun. He looks around, then breathes a sigh of relief that he's still alive. The ship deck sways gently as the man moves over to his female companions, huddled together, tearfully trembling in terror. They watch apprehensively as Rasmus walks deliberately to the bow of the yacht and looks out, gazing to the open horizon.

The assembled yacht crew and staff are gathered close together under threat of violence. Everyone watches as a crewman is escorted down the stairway from the cabin above. He is forcibly marched to the front of the ship toward the waiting air pirate captain. One of the mercenary crew pushes the white-uniformed deckhand forward and holds out an old-fashioned, double-barreled shotgun to Rasmus.

"Sir, this is the man who shot Kwan."

Rasmus takes hold of the antique shotgun and gives it a quick inspection. He presses the breach lever aside with his thumb, breaks the barrels open, and dumps out the two spent twelve-gauge shells. They fall to the wooden deck with a clank and roll to the side. Extending it out, Rasmus offers the shotgun to the dismayed crewman who takes it reluctantly.

"Load it for me. Both barrels."

The yacht crewman looks confused as the pirate next to him holds two fresh shotgun shells in his open palm. He looks at the offered loads, then over at the pirate leader. With a malevolent stare, the air captain waits, watching the crewman as he stands frozen in fear.

Rasmus raises the Lugar pistol for extra motivation. "What's the matter? You obviously know how to use it."

The yacht crewman slowly takes the two target pigeon shells and loads the shotgun. He looks up at Rasmus, who nods his consent, and the crewman snaps the barrels shut. Stepping forward, Rasmus switches his Lugar pistol to his off hand and reaches out. "Now hand it to me. The stock first."

Slowly, the crewman turns the shotgun around and holds it out away from himself. Rasmus looks down at the weapon offered and responds, "A mite further, so you can see what my good man over there saw before you executed him."

The crewman extends the shotgun out a bit more and looks down at the business-end of the smooth-bore barrels. Rasmus turns to face the owner of the yacht, and his features turn hard. "Sir, is this your shotgun?"

"I, uh... I use it for skeet shooting."

"Did Kwan look like a sporting target?"

Rasmus carefully wraps his hand around the wooden stock of the shotgun and slips his finger into the metal guard. His finger slides across the ready trigger and feels the tension. "Now, having guns around can get people into real trouble, or even worse... *Hurt*."

Unflinchingly, Rasmus pulls the trigger on the shotgun. The explosive blast at point-blank range sends the crewman in front of it reeling back across the ship deck. The pirate captain walks forward and stands over the crewman lying in a heap. His features fierce and unrelenting, Rasmus turns and waves the other loaded barrel of the shotgun at the assembled crew.

"Now, I would like everyone to please move to the bow of this sinking ship."

One of the bikini-clad women gasps and stutters, in wide-eyed dismay. "But, it's not s-s-sinking..."

With a sweeping gesture, Rasmus raises his hand, points the shotgun at the liquor cart, and unleashes the other loaded barrel. The explosion of bottle glass and shattered spirits sends a frightening amount of debris across the deck. Rasmus tosses the shotgun aside as he looks over the pleasure yacht and its cluster of occupants. "It soon will be."

An evil smile creeps across Rasmus's cold features as the air pirate crew quickly goes to work.

Chapter 3

Nestled in the isles of the South Pacific, to the east of the war-torn Philippine territories, sit the remote Polynesian Islands of Samoa. On one of the many smaller atolls near Safata Bay is a jungled piece of land, with an inlet on one side that leads to a large lagoon. Long trunks of swaying palms extend out over the dark sandy shores.

In the lagoon, tied to the end of a rickety constructed dock, floats a large, post-war Grumman seaplane. Two Pratt & Whitney nine-cylinder radial engines gleam in the broken sunlight, with the casing behind them blackened from the exhaust of heavy use. The stepped-hull body of the flying boat sits low in the water with the high, single wing extending past the dock and supported on the calm glimmering surface by the wingtip floats.

Upon closer inspection, repaired bullet holes scar the riveted panels near the pilot-side window of the floating white-and-blue water-bird. The rear hatch, just forward of the tail section, sits open, with crates of supplies on the dock ready for loading. There is nary a ripple on the surface of the lagoon, and, from the dense tropical foliage, the sound of insects and native bird chatter fills the air.

Several yards away, across a patch of overgrown jungle, a wide, sandy beach stretches around to the mouth of the inlet. Growing out over the strand, swaying trunks of palm trees, topped with shaggy green fronds, reach for blue skies and sun. Hanging between two of the palm trees swings a small half-scale hammock.

A soft, purring snore escapes from the canvas shell, and the lanky, hair-covered arm of a monkey drapes over the side. A medium-sized primate, native to Indo-China, Curtiss grunts and readjusts in the hanging bed. Being a faithful companion, Curtiss serves as friend and copilot to the owner of the Grumman seaplane docked nearby.

Not far from the sleeping copilot swings a full-sized U.S. Navy military surplus hammock. From it, two furry human arms hang over the side with fingertips skimming just over the warm, debris-littered sand. Strewn on the beach surrounding the hammocks are several empty beer bottles, a half-bottle of rum, and various pieces of clothing, including a petite bikini.

Small waves roll and lap gently onto the sandy beach. Splashing sounds a few yards out in the clear waters bring attention to a native island girl swimming to shore with long, black hair trailing behind her. She dives under the surface and comes up again, smoothing her dark hair away from her strikingly sculpted features.

Pushing back to a floating position, her youthful breasts break the surface of the water and mound up to point skyward. Kicking, she turns her head as the sound of reverberating airplane engines are heard in the distance.

A pair of black PBY Catalina seaplanes fly low, roaring over the calm, aqua-blue waters on approach to the island. The rumbling thunder of their powerful engines momentarily silences the chatter of noisy insects and squawking birds. From the hammock, a shaggy, unkempt head of hair rises at the shoulders to watch the two warplanes fly in tight formation overhead. His curiosity is held a moment, before his sun-bronzed shoulders collapse down again in slumber.

Living on the islands of the South Pacific since his release from military service after the Second World War, James "Jimmy" Ferral has assimilated to the overseas lifestyle. A veteran U.S. Navy pilot and part-time recluse, he is the proud owner of an independent air charter operation run out of the island shack adjacent to the lagoon. His life seems uncomplicated, managing his own schedule, with the assistance of a fuzzy simian copilot and an acquired military surplus seaplane.

Jimmy, tanned and rugged-looking from outdoor living, lifts his head again and watches the swimming woman out in the waves. Her smiling gaze meets his, and she dives under the surface, kicking toward him. In waist-high water, she stands. The warm ocean wetness rolls off her exposed, golden body, as she splashes toward the beach.

The breeze blows gently, rattling the unkempt fronds on the palm trees above. Jimmy rests his head to the side of the hammock and watches, as she strolls toward him and pulls a towel from the line. A content grunt escapes his lips, then he drops his head back into the slung canvas bed. Glistening naked, she pats her hair dry then sits on the suspended hammock next to him.

"Jimmy, you can't sleep all day."

He rolls over to reveal a man who, from the length of his hair and beard stubble, appears to have gone native.

"I bet I could."

"Well, *I* can't. I have a job."

"Yeah, I have one of those, too... Sometimes…"

Kicking her feet out, she swings the canvas hammock. "Well, Mister Island-hopper, I have to get back for my shift."

"Or you could just stay here a while longer?"

She leans down and gives him a sweet, pecking kiss. "You don't want me to be late for work, do you?"

She slides from the hammock and nimbly bends down to pick up her bikini pieces. She shakes the sand out and steps into the bottoms. "You're still coming in for dinner this afternoon, aren't you? You promised you would before your next charter delivery."

Jimmy scratches his head and looks around. "Yeah, I'll be there. I just have to, uh, wait for Curtiss."

As she untangles the strings on her swimsuit top, she looks at the passed-out monkey in the hammock.

"Why do you let him drink so much?"

"I can't decide how he spends his money."

Adjusting her swim suit, the native girl looks up to see a female stranger's arrival at the office shack near the lagoon.

Dressed in khaki pants, boots, and a thin white T-shirt, Alexa Reid is an archaeologist and experienced adventurer. Her very elegant and attractive exterior hides a hardened and ruthlessly ambitious core. She notices the occupied hammocks near the shoreline and, with a confident stride, walks under the scattered palm trees down the path to the beach.

The native girl nods to Jimmy, as she ties her floral-patterned sarong and suspiciously watches the approaching woman. "Better throw some pants on. You have a visitor."

She snaps her fingers across his naked bottom then drops a towel on Jimmy, which he wraps around his waist as Alexa steps up. With her emerald-colored eyes, the attractive stranger looks over the island pair, and then glances to the smaller hammock before resuming her attentive stare.

"Captain James Ferral?"

Jimmy struggles to sit upright in the hammock.

"That's correct. What can I do you for?"

"I need to speak to you about a job."

The world seems to spin a bit and become fuzzy, as the seaplane pilot rubs his temples and tries to tame his wild hair. Jimmy coughs and clears his throat with a laugh. "I'm not hiring today... Sorry."

Alexa rolls her eyes and subtly shakes her head, as she looks at the nearly naked man in the hammock and the bikini-clad female alongside. She turns to the primitive island surroundings and nearly second guesses her objective, until she sets eyes on the high-winged Grumman seaplane peacefully docked in the lagoon. "Maybe you could put on some undershorts, and we could speak business in private."

Reaching out, Jimmy pats the native girl on the bottom. "Darlin', could you please excuse us. See you in the village."

The girl leans down and gives Jimmy a long, deeply passionate kiss. She pretends not to notice Alexa watching as she runs her nimble fingers along his naked, suntanned body. As she comes up for air, her eyes dart to the female interloper, then back to Jimmy. "See you in town, Jimmy."

She gives Alexa a possessive glare and ambles with a hip-tossing strut toward the ramshackle hut near the dock. Alexa watches as the girl mounts an old rusty bicycle that was leaned against the wall and pedals off down the dirt path.

Perched on the edge of the hammock, Jimmy watches the island girl ride away and then turns to Alexa, as he rubs the graying whisker-stubble on his cheek. "Well... Would you like to talk business here or in my office?"

Alexa stares at Jimmy, who gestures to the bamboo and wooden surplus-crate constructed hut. She seems unamused, as she scans the empty beach cautiously. "Here would be fine. Are we alone?"

"Yep, except for Curtiss."

"Who?" Her eyes dart over to the office shack and seaplane dock, searching for another person.

"My copilot. Shhh, he's asleep."

With a half-drunken wink, Jimmy nods toward the smaller hammock hung nearby. Alexa gives Jimmy a scrutinizing stare. "Captain Ferral, are you intoxicated?"

He looks around, as if not sure. "Nooo, why?"

"I need a pilot, and I need a good one. Not someone who is going to be..." Alexa glances over at Curtiss, as the monkey copilot snorts a snore and rolls sunny-side up while scratching his furry belly. "...*monkeying around,* shall I say? Are you any good?"

Trying to blink his vision clear, Jimmy straightens up a bit and gets more serious. He grips the edge of the hammock and sets his jaw. "I was good enough to make it through a World War, flying air transports and rescues in heavy combat. I guess I'm good enough for whatever you have in mind."

Alexa shrugs and continues. "Well then..."

Jimmy puts a hand up and motions for her to be silent. "Hold on there, Missy. Let's back up a bit, shall we. First of all, who the hell are you?" He pauses a moment and studies her form-fitting outfit, then looks up to the fine bone structure of her features and her long, wavy hair pulled loosely back. Staring for a second too long, he shakes his head and returns to his rant. "Secondly, what is so damned important that you come out to this nowhere island and need this great world-class pilot?"

Alexa squats in the sand before Jimmy and looks over her shoulder down the beach. She turns back and gracefully swooshes the hair away from her face, distracting the woozy seaplane pilot again.

Jimmy clears his throat and points a finger skyward. "And third... Uh, I forgot what's third."

Shifting her position, dropping to her knees in the sand, Alexa gives Jimmy a gentle smile.

"I'm sorry. My name is Alexa Reid. You may have read about me in the papers."

Jimmy looks around at the desolate island paradise. "Uhmm, no. I haven't received my paper subscription to the *New York Times* in a while."

"I'm an archaeologist of sorts, and I need your services to fly me to a small uncharted island not far from here."

Standing slowly from the hammock, Jimmy feels the blood pressure in his head, due to alcohol-induced abuse. "There are a lot of small uncharted islands around these parts. That's not so difficult."

"Yes, just important."

Jimmy's towel starts to slip, and he adjusts it, trying to keep it wrapped. His head pounding with drinker's remorse, he bends to pick up his clothes. "When do you need to go? Next week is open for me."

Alexa stands and brushes the sand from her knees. "Can we leave right now?"

He winces and looks up at her as if she is joking. Straightening and shaking the sand from his shorts and shirt, he glances at her with a dazed expression.

"Now? What's the big hurry?"

"I thought you were a charter pilot for hire?"

"I am, but I don't do anything *right now*."

"You will be well paid."

Jimmy tucks his clothes under his arm and wags his head. "Forget it, I've got plans tonight. I don't know what the newspapers say, but you've got more money than manners."

Slightly irritated, Alexa again changes her approach. With a renewed sense of urgency, she addresses Jimmy. "Captain Ferral, this is a very important mission. It's a matter of life and death."

Jimmy stumbles down the path to his island shack and stops to look over his shoulder. "Life and death for who?"

Alexa takes a measured breath and walks toward him. "For both of us."

Jimmy tilts his head, confused but attentive.

Chapter 4

The ramshackle office dwelling at the end of the pier clatters and bangs like a gang of rampant cats is brawling inside. Jimmy races out the door and piles a handful of supplies on the dock near the rear hatch of the tethered flying boat. Standing nearby, Alexa waits with a backpack and medium canvas duffle. He glares over at her, highly annoyed, and races back into the shack.

Jimmy momentarily sticks his head out to gape at her. He shakes his head, staggering for the right words, and ducks back inside to finally yell out through the opened window. "So, you're saying... Even if I don't take you, they'll shoot me and deep six my plane, just so you don't leave this island?"

Alexa watches Jimmy exit the hut with another sack full of supplies and toss it into the seaplane's rear cargo hatch. "That's right."

He huffs, runs back into the shack, and quickly returns with a short-barreled '97 trench-gun, a 1911 automatic pistol, and a shot-shell cartridge belt draped over his shoulder. Jimmy jacks the fore-stock pump on the shotgun and checks the empty chamber.

"It's a sure bet they'll kill me if I do take you."

He sets down the shotgun and the belt of twelve-gauge cartridges, and then he pulls back the slide on the handgun, chambering a round.

Alexa smiles at him meekly. "Probably."

Jimmy lets the slide slam back and clicks on the safety. "So, I guess, it's you win and I'm screwed."

"You have to understand these men."

He turns and waves the auto pistol toward her angrily. "Wrong, I don't have to understand them. They're probably about as wacko as you. If you're conning me or spinning tales so I'll take you, I'll murder you myself."

Unintimidated, Alexa ignores the gun and stares straight at Jimmy. "Captain, you will be well paid."

Tucking the loaded pistol into one of the bags, he fastens the leather straps. "You're damn right I will be."

~*~

The Grumman flying-boat sits patiently rocking in the lagoon, as Jimmy loads supplies through the rear hatch door. Alexa sits inside the seaplane on an empty wooden crate with Curtiss lying prone across her lap, getting his belly rubbed. Jimmy looks at his copilot blissfully lounging, and he shakes his head in disgust. "Curtiss, you have no idea what kind of trouble that woman is getting us into."

Alexa rubs the monkey under the chin and then looks up at Jimmy. "If you don't hurry with what you're doing and get us out of here, we might be in trouble."

"Lady, I'm not flying over hundreds of miles of water and uninhabited islands without a few supplies."

Jimmy stops with one foot inside the rocking seaplane and one still on the wooden dock, as he suddenly turns his complete attention skyward. The distinctive sound of multiple airplane engines can be heard approaching in the distance. Alexa identifies the recognizable sound of the pirate seaplanes and jumps to her feet, tossing Curtiss away from her lap. "That's them! We have to get out of here, now!"

Disturbed from his rest, Curtiss quickly climbs up to a netted nest in the corner of the cargo area and peers out. Jimmy listens for a moment, then drops what is in his hands and sternly looks to Alexa. "Stay put."

Dashing out of the seaplane cargo door, he runs to the end of the dock and watches as the two Catalina seaplanes pass overhead. He runs down the dock, grabs the shotgun and cartridge belt full of twelve-gauge shells, and looks up again. The post-war surplus airplanes circle once and then approach for a water landing near the mouth of the lagoon.

"Shit... Shit!" Jimmy runs back to the Grumman seaplane as the first PBY Catalina seaplane touches down on the water and glides toward the beach.

Obscured by the shadows, Alexa stands and watches inside the hatch. Jimmy pushes her aside and climbs in. She follows him to the front of the cargo hold and observes as he starts to shuffle through piles of gear.

"Now can we get out of here?"

"No..."

"We can't stay here."

He looks over his shoulder at her and shakes his head. "We're not going anywhere. Those PBY Catalinas are military *Black Cat* warplanes. I saw fifty caliber guns on the side blisters and twin thirties in the nose turret. They could shoot us right out of the sky in a heartbeat."

"You don't seem to understand yet, Captain."

"What don't I understand?"

"They are going to kill you if they catch me."

Jimmy moves another crate and pulls on one of the interior panels of the wall. "You mentioned that."

The cavity in the seaplane's hull houses the mechanism for the retracted wheel struts and enough space for a person. He turns to grab hold of Alexa and shoves his unwelcome visitor into the narrow nook. The tight space can barely fit her, but he nods, approvingly, as he picks up the pump shotgun. "Time to get small."

"What are you doing?"

Jimmy thumbs shells into the underside of the sawed-off shotgun and then looks at Alexa, as she adjusts herself in the cramped space. "They're not going to find you in here. Stay in there until I come for you." Jimmy gives the shotgun a pump and tosses the ammo belt aside. He hands her the firearm and gives a smile. "If anyone other than me opens this panel, blast 'em."

In dismayed shock, Alexa looks at Jimmy while he replaces the secret cargo wall-section and closes her up inside. He quickly piles supplies in front of the hidden panel, carefully concealing Alexa's hiding place.

~*~

The two pirate Catalina seaplanes idle their engines, coasting to the beach and the narrow inlet of the large lagoon. Once in position to block the exit from the sheltered cove, the big radial engines chug to a halt, and the floating hulls drift to a smooth-bottom landing through the gentle rolling waves. The three-bladed props rotate slowly and then cease movement. There is a brief calm in the air before the hatches and doors on the two seaplanes swing open.

The assembly of air pirates climb from the flying boats, move through the shallow surf and onto the sandy shore. Automatic rifles slung over their shoulders and pistols held at the ready, the seaplane pirates spread out and secure the area. The dozens of machine-gun laden men extending along the exotic shoreline makes for a very uninviting day at the beach.

Jimmy walks down the narrow dirt path from his island shack toward the shore as he tucks his slab-sided .45-auto pistol into his waistband behind his back, under his shirt. He peruses the occupied beach while assessing the headcount and visible firepower of the pirate group. "Hello there, boys. Haven't seen Catalinas like these since the war."

The friendly greeting is met by cold, vacant stares, as the mercenary crew continues to spread out along the beach. Intrigued, Jimmy stands and watches, as all eyes suddenly drift toward the pirate seaplane nearest the shore. From the hatch, Captain P. M. Rasmus steps out and pays no heed to his shoes or linen pants as he plods through the shallow surf.

The flying-boat captain walks up onto the beach, tips back his gray fedora hat and touches a probing finger under his black leather eye-patch. Rasmus scans his good eye along the beachfront and stares at Jimmy standing near the edge of the jungle. He walks toward him with an air of strange civility. "Good afternoon. Captain James Ferral, I presume?"

Jimmy nods as Rasmus walks up the shoreline toward him and extends his hand. They exchange a firm handshake, and Jimmy tries to relax despite the uncomfortable encounter. "My friends call me Jimmy."

Rasmus gives a pleasant smile and looks over Jimmy's shoulder toward the white-and-blue amphibious seaplane tethered along the dock in the lagoon. He eyes the pile of supplies still on the pier and the flying boat resting at an oddly canted position in the water. "Captain Ferral, er... Jimmy is it? My name is Captain P. M. Rasmus, and I believe we have a few business matters to discuss."

Jimmy looks around at the surrounding army of pirates occupying his home turf. Though seemingly nonaggressive at the moment, each appears ready for action and well-armed. He studies the one-eyed, flying-boat captain before him and gives a feeble shrug.

"Step into my office."

~*~

The evening sun dips lower, and the ramshackle hut sits in the shadows of the surrounding jungle. Down along the beachfront, groups of pirates lounge in clusters around small fire pits dug in the sand. A lit oil torch at the end of the dock casts an orange flaming light on parts of the lagoon and reflects off the port side of the floating seaplane.

Illuminated by a squat, melting candle, Jimmy and Rasmus sit across from each other at a table outside the hut. About halfway through a bottle of rum, Jimmy offers another pour to Rasmus, which is declined. The pirate sits straight in his chair and examines Jimmy with his single, clear eye.

"You say the woman stopped this morning?"

Swaying in his seat with obvious drunkenness, Jimmy looks over at his monkey copilot sitting on a chair next to him. The furry primate is firmly holding a rum-filled glass tumbler, in which he is continually dipping and then licking his finger. Jimmy looks back to Rasmus.

"Huh?"

"The woman?"

"Yeah?"

"When, exactly, did she approach you?"

"She came late morning, afternoon, something like that. Probably two or three hours before you landed my beach."

The pirate captain looks at the silhouetted seaplane in the lagoon and lets his piercing eye travel over to the pile of supplies near the rear hatch. "Your cargo area is loaded for a journey. Why did you decline her business offer?"

Jimmy takes a sip of rum and lets the warmth of the liquor settle in. "I'm headed out on a delivery run and her plans didn't fit into my busy schedule." The expat American chuckles to himself, amused at his own mention of any sort of timetable or calendar.

"Did she reveal her plans?"

"Doesn't matter, I'm booked."

Studying Jimmy intently, Rasmus probes for any semblance of truth from the increasingly drunk pilot. "You know where she went after you turned her down?"

Jimmy smiles and lounges back in the chair with his glass of rum. He gives it a swirl and glances over at Curtiss. "Nope, I told her to go back to the village and find someone. She likely ended up renting one of the boats for hire there."

Noticing Rasmus's eye wander to the seaplane again, Jimmy dumps out most of his rum glass to the ground and brings it up to his lips as if still drinking. The pirate brings his attention back to the seaplane pilot and Jimmy raises his glass high in a toasting gesture. "Appreciate the drinks 'nd all... But, like I told you before... I have to pick up some cargo in Fiji to take over to the Tonga Trench."

Rasmus scrutinizes Jimmy prudently and seems to lose his feigned humor. "When my men return with the woman, you can leave. Until then, I'll compensate you for your time."

"Yeah, how's that?"

The pirate captain pulls a leather pouch from his coat pocket and carefully opens it. He shakes three gold coins into his hand and places them each on the table with a snap. Rasmus secures the string closure on the pouch and returns it to his jacket pocket, as he watches the pilot gawk wide-eyed over the ancient coins.

Jimmy looks from the money up to Rasmus and smirks. "I can wait as long as you need."

~*~

The bottle of rum is nearly empty. Curtiss snores, sleeping with his furry head drooped to the side of the table. Rasmus sits perfectly straight in his chair and finishes his glass of libation. The light from the candle reflects in his eye.

Jimmy leans in with his elbows on the table and casts a heavy-lidded, sozzled gaze to the patch-wearing, flying-boat captain seated across from him. He tries to concentrate his vision with a rum-soaked focus. "Why is it you need this gal? Kinda young for you... She your girl or somethin'?"

Rasmus remains poised, but he's irritated with his lack of progress. "Captain Ferral, my business with this woman is of a personal nature."

Jimmy drunkenly reaches out and takes hold of Rasmus's forearm. "I get it. You want her as your lady-friend? Not much personality, but nice..." As Jimmy mumbles out his last words, his head slumps to the table and he passes out.

Unsympathetic, Rasmus firmly removes Jimmy's hand from his person and sits staring at the drunken aviator before him. "For your sake, I hope you know nothing about her..." Rasmus stands, looming over the small table, with the flickering light from the candle glowing on his hard features. He looks from Jimmy face down on the table, then to the sleeping monkey copilot spread out on a chair quietly snoring, and continues menacingly, "...or tomorrow your hangover will be the least of your pains."

The distinguished one-eyed gentleman in the fedora shakes his head despondently and steps away from the table. Rasmus stands at the edge of the jungle path and looks out over the starry reflections on the mirrored surface of the lagoon.

"Where are you, girl?"

The ivory-colored suit he wears glows in the darkness, as Rasmus strides down the dirt path toward the beachfront. He walks past the few remaining fires on the beach, looks out to the seaplanes nosed in the sand and disappears into the moonlit shadows. The quiet lapping of waves fills the air.

Chapter 5

The moon rises to midnight and bathes the lagoon in a pale blue light. The squat candle on the table and the oil torches along the wooden dock still flicker with a soft amber glow. Face down on the table top, Jimmy rolls his head to the side. He opens one eye slowly, followed cautiously by the other. The shadows from the jungle remain still, and when Jimmy senses no one is nearby, he quietly taps his copilot awake. "Curtiss, check around. See if anyone is watching."

The primate copilot sits up and sleepily rubs his eyes. He climbs down from the comfort of the chair and ambles off into the darkness. Jimmy lifts his head slightly and looks around the best he can. After a while, he feels a tap on his leg. He looks down to see Curtiss with a wide, toothy grin and a German pistol clenched in his mitts. Jimmy takes the gun from his monkey companion and pats him on the shoulder.

"Good job. Let's get out of here."

The absconding pilot and monkey cohort quietly move down the wooden dock, while Jimmy unfastens the seaplane from the tie-down cleats. The soft creak of rubber bumpers against the painted metal hull squeak into the quiet night, as the shifting weight causes the dock to rub on the airframe. Curtiss scampers in through the rear hatch and Jimmy gathers up the rope ties and tosses them inside. He gives the seaplane a soft shove from the dock, steps inside the cargo hatch door, and closes it quietly behind him.

In the darkness, Jimmy dashes to the front of the aircraft and slides behind the left seat controls. As they slowly drift away, he pushes his side window open and looks out at the familiar old dock. The seconds tick by, as Jimmy takes a minute to complete the preflight checklist. He glances over at his furry copilot, takes a deep breath, and prepares to fire up the two large radial engines.

"This is it, pal."

At the mouth of the lagoon, pirates lay on the beach, camping in the warm night air. Glowing embers from the evening's fires still twinkle in the sand and give off the aroma of palm and burned coconut. Across the dark sheltered cove, the sudden roar of the twin radial engines bursting to life explodes through the calm, quiet night. The pirates leap from their slumber and grab their nearby firearms.

Nudging the overhead throttles forward, Jimmy taxies the seaplane to the far edge of the dark waters of the lagoon. He pulls back on the left engine throttle and gooses the starboard engine to turn the water-bird on a dime. Pointed out to the mouth of the island cove and open waters ahead, Jimmy pulls back the right throttle and matches the two rumbling engines for idle power.

The moonlit beach is a hurried mass of commotion and movement, as every pirate is called to immediate action. Scrambling down the path toward the lagoon, the air pirates keep their guns directed out before them. The landing lights on the two PBY Catalina seaplanes suddenly snap on and flood the beach with an intense white light.

At the controls of the Grumman flying boat, Jimmy stares out over the dark, dancing shadows on the lagoon. Through the leafy jungle along the coastline, the bright lights of the two pirate Catalina seaplanes can be seen near the mouth of the inlet. He shakes his head and glances over at Curtiss in the copilot's chair.

"Here we go, buddy... "

Jimmy reaches up and pushes the overhead throttles forward, making both radial engines roar with combustion. The seaplane slowly begins to nose ahead, plowing through the water. He adjusts the throttles again to match the engines for power and keep on a straight line of departure.

Picking up speed, water sprays from under the curved bow and churns through the tips of the spinning propellers. Steadily pulling back on the yoke, Jimmy eases the seaplane up onto the stepped hull. Gliding across the lagoon, the seaplane appears to be skipping across a sheet of dark glass.

As the amphibious flying boat approaches the inlet, Jimmy peers into the darkness and flips the ACL switch. Outside, the aircraft landing lights on the

Grumman seaplane suddenly flash on and the water path is brightly illuminated. Directly in front of them, at the cove's exit, Jimmy and Curtiss see one of the Catalina pirate seaplanes, with idling engines, jockeying to an attack position.

Curtiss stands in the copilot's chair and points toward the fast-approaching profile of the pirate Catalina, jumping and screeching in warning. Jimmy eases back the yoke, and the seaplane increases water speed as it rises higher on the step, like a speedboat at full throttle. The staccato sound of automatic gunshots echoes across the lagoon, and Jimmy looks over as some of the pirates hurry to the end of the dock.

Flashes of light pop in unison as the pirates fire their weapons at the escaping seaplane, racing across the water. Several hot rounds of lead tear into the thin metal airframe. The twin radial engines scream with the strain of liftoff, as the boat-plane begins to rise from the water.

Finally maneuvered to an attack position, the black PBY Catalina sits crosswise at the mouth of the inlet leading into the lagoon. The nose hatch swings open and Rasmus emerges, lit from below like a dark, one-eyed demon. He watches the bright lights of the Grumman seaplane as they speed across the lagoon, traveling straight toward him. Just toward the tail of the Catalina, the large caliber blister gun positions and zeros in on its approaching target.

Jimmy clenches his teeth as the Grumman seaplane bears down on the pirate Catalina. Curtiss puts his furry hands over his eyes and screeches. Feet braced on the elevator pedals, Jimmy glances over at Curtiss, then down at the speed indicator, while pulling back on the yoke with all his strength.

"C'mon baby, give me all ya got!"

Several shots blast from the Catalina's side-blister turret, and lit tracers whiz past the engines of the high-winged seaplane as it moves within range of the attacking pirates. Finally lifting from the lagoon, freed from its bond with the surface of the water, the Grumman seaplane roars skyward over the obstructing pirate Catalina. The men on the ground continue firing on the airborne vessel until its landing lights blink out, becoming a mere, fading roar in the night sky.

~*~

Standing in the forward nose hatch, looking up to the star-filled firmament and unable to follow into the heavens, Captain Rasmus hammers his fist on the nose of the warplane. The large fifty caliber blister gun ceases fire, and the bright tracers fade into the darkness. The pirates moving along the beach slowly cease fire, and the night is enveloped with an uncomfortable stillness.

The landing lights from the two pirate seaplanes remain lit, illuminating the empty camps along the beach. Rasmus looks out across the lagoon to the flickering glow of the oil lamps still burning on the vacant dock and utters, "Captain Ferral. You've done a very stupid thing, for which you will pay dearly."

Rasmus lingers in the hatch and stares skyward. Illuminated by the interior lights coming from below, his features seem to burn with a vengeful menace.

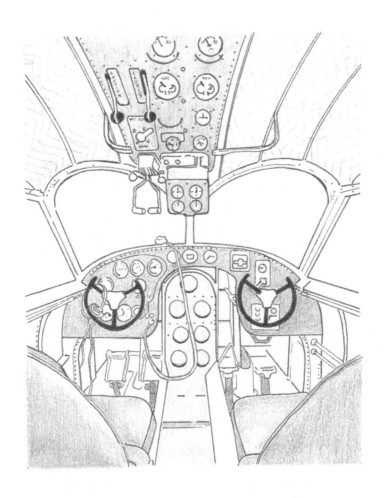

Chapter 6

In the darkness of the Grumman seaplane fuselage, Jimmy fumbles with a flashlight. The beam of light finally flicks on, and he scans around the cluttered interior of the cargo hold. The engines rumble through the sky with a steady rhythm, as he moves boxes and crates away from the area in front of the false panel. Jimmy eventually finds the hidden latch and pulls the concealed wall-section free. The shotgun is instantly thrust to his midsection, doubling him over and causing him to drop the flashlight.

A swift uppercut of the shotgun's wooden stock catches Jimmy across the cheek, as he grabs hold of Alexa and pulls her from the cavity. He knocks the shotgun from her hands and tackles her to the floor. Jimmy struggles to hold her down, and she swings out, connecting her clenched fist to his nose. He yelps from the pain, as he grabs at her wrists.

"Stop it! What the hell are you doing?"

As he finally restrains her, the loose flashlight rolls across the floor to reveal Jimmy sitting atop Alexa.

She looks up and appears genuinely surprised to see Jimmy, with a trickle of blood running from his nostril. "Captain Ferral? Is that you?"

Jimmy continues to pin her to the floor and winces at his sore nose. "Who were you expecting?"

"Who is flying the airplane?"

He relaxes his grip a bit and sits back on his haunches. Jimmy smiles at her reassuringly. "Curtiss... "

Eyes opening wide, Alexa struggles to free herself from his grasp, and Jimmy pushes forward to restrain her again. She screams out and sputters with angry frustration. "What? A *monkey* is flying the airplane? You reek like you're drunk... Let go of me! I want out of here!"

"Relax! It's dark... He can't see anything outside anyway. And I'm not drunk."

Alexa struggles, while Jimmy holds her fists. He gives her a shake and puts all his weight on her wrists.

"I'll let you up, if you promise not to hit me."

"Just get to the controls and pilot this thing!"

Jimmy releases Alexa's hands, but still sits atop her. Touching his nose, he winces from the pain.

"You've got quite the hook."

"If you don't get off me and fly this airplane, there will be another coming your way."

He raises a hand and wags a warning finger.

"Hey, you promised."

Alexa makes a clenched fist, and Jimmy quickly hops off of her. He grabs the flashlight and snaps back the secretive panel. Alexa looks ahead toward the nearly empty cockpit and back at Jimmy. "Anything else you would like to tidy up back here before resuming control of this aircraft, Captain Ferral?"

Jimmy looks at her and smiles before moving toward the front of the airplane.

"Nope, that should do it for now."

Alexa takes a deep, calming breath and follows.

~*~

The Grumman seaplane flies through the stillness of night with only the moon, clouds and stars guiding the way. In the vast emptiness below, the shimmer of the heavens reflects on the dark ocean waters. Alexa sits in the copilot's chair with Curtiss asleep across her lap. She looks out the starboard window, then over at Jimmy. He watches forward, with the green lights of the instrument panel reflected on his seasoned features.

"Thank you."

"For which part?" he asks, staring ahead.

"Getting me out of there alive."

He turns his gaze slightly toward her, but remains focused on the stars' navigational arrangement in the night sky. "My pleasure."

He touches his sore nose and returns to gazing forward. Alexa pets Curtiss a little and glances out the window again. "I am sorry about hitting you. How was I supposed to know?" She sees his reflection in the dark glass and adds, "You left me in there, for I don't know how long, fearing for my life."

Jimmy looks over at her and can't help but notice the simple beauty of her features, enhanced by the instrument panel's glow and the silvery moonlight.

"Yeah, I should've said something."

She smiles warmly at him and pets the monkey copilot. "Yes, Captain Ferral, it is customary for a gentleman to announces himself before pulling a damsel in distress from a cramped, smuggler's compartment."

Jimmy nods, amused, while adjusting one of the lit up dials in front of him. "You can call me Jimmy."

He glances down at the island map tucked into the side pouch along his seat cushion. He slides it out and unfolds the chart across his lap. With a small penlight held in his mouth, he studies it and mumbles aside to her.

"Okay, damsel in distress. We've been heading west for the past little while and should be clear of your unfriendly cohorts. Now, where exactly are we going?"

"Are you sure they aren't following us?"

"Do they know which island you're going to?"

"I am the only one with the exact coordinates."

Jimmy looks out the side window, then over at her. "Listen, I don't really enjoy flying this bird at night, because... You know what, it's not very safe landing on a dark body of water that is mirroring the night sky." Jimmy takes the flashlight from his mouth to hold it. "That fellow Rasmus and his air-pirates won't be going anywhere until morning, because the odds of successfully following us at night are, well... They're not very good. Now, what is the name of that island you want to get to?"

"I don't know if it has a name."

Jimmy smirks at her elusive answer. "If it's on the map, it has a name."

He watches, as Alexa pulls a folded piece of paper from her breast-pocket. She unfolds the small note and scans it before passing it to Jimmy. "These are the coordinates. It's not an island on any of those charts."

Holding the flashlight in his mouth again, Jimmy takes the folded piece of paper and studies the numbers against their positioning on the map. He circles his finger on the general location and sighs. "There are hundreds of uncharted islands in the area."

Alexa reaches over and takes the coordinates from him. "That's why I need you to fly me there."

The small flashlight drops from Jimmy's mouth, and he clicks it off. "What I mean is that some of those uncharted land masses are above water one year and below it the next."

"Well Captain, these are the directions to just one in particular."

"What do you think is going to be on this uncharted island?"

"I just need you to get me there to have a look and then fly me back to civilization."

The airplane is seemingly stationary as it flies along in the night sky. Jimmy shrugs. "That's what I do."

"And that's what I will pay you for."

The two sit in silence awhile, listening to the steady rumble of the synchronized radial engines. The glow from the instrument panel reflects off the windows and puts heavy shadows across their features. Jimmy looks to Alexa as she yawns and lays back her head.

"Use the bunk in back. You should sleep."

Alexa turns to Jimmy for a moment, then stands and gently puts the slumbering copilot back on the cushioned seat. She pats the snoring monkey, as he curls up comfortably in his own chair. At the door to the cargo area, Alexa puts her hand on Jimmy's shoulder as she passes. "Thank you again, Jimmy."

He nods and glances up at her, as she disappears into the cargo hold of the airplane. Fine-tuning the flight controls, he listens as she settles into the creaking, military-style bunk. The blackness outside seems endless, as he casts an eye to his sleeping copilot snuffling quietly, contented with dreams of bananas and rum drinks.

"What did you get me into?"

Chapter 7

The amphibious flying boat sits moored in a crowded island harbor amongst several other floating yachts and sailboats. Jimmy sits atop the high wing above a refueling vessel and watches, as a young native boy fills the tanks on the seaplane. He leans back on his hands and stares out over the numerous styles of boats in the sheltered bay while breathing in the slightly petrol-tainted air.

The young boy tops off the seaplane and replaces the fuel nozzle on the tanker. Jimmy breaks from his rumination and walks down the seaplane's wings to inspect the job.

"Thanks, kid. Write me up a receipt for the fill-up, and I'll take care of it at Charlie's."

Jimmy carefully steps down over the windshield of the flying boat to the nose hatch, and the young boy hands him a bill of sale for the fuel. Jimmy takes the paper and jams it into his pocket, then unties the tanker vessel from the nose cleat. Waving, the native kid motors away, as Alexa peeks out the rear cargo-window. She peers around curiously and leans out farther to see Jimmy at the nose hatch, coiling a length of rope.

"Jimmy?"

Sliding down into the nose compartment, Jimmy crawls through into the cockpit and moves back to the cargo area.

"Good morning. Glad to see you're refreshed."

"What are we doing here, Jimmy? We can't stop here. We have to get going."

Jimmy steps back and scowls at her, instantly annoyed. "Whoa! Relax... We needed fuel to keep this bird in the sky."

Alexa looks nervously out the window at the crowded harbor, and Jimmy pushes past her to the single bunk setup opposite the rear hatch opening. He sits on the narrow bed, mumbles to himself and begins to untie the laces on his leather ankle boots. She moves over to the bunk and stands before him with authority.

"You didn't tell anyone where we are going?"

"Should I have?"

"I am serious, Captain Ferral. No one can know where we are headed, and we surely can't be here!"

Jimmy tugs off one boot and unties the other. "So now it's *Captain* again? Tell me, why can't we be here?"

Alexa turns away and looks out the windows on the seaplane, anxiously. "Those men we left behind last night are not going to just stop. They have contacts and spies all over these islands. It won't be long until they find us."

The bunk creaks, as Jimmy leans back to pull his other boot off. He tosses it aside and puts his hand up to quiet her.

"I flew all damn night just to be a safe distance from those guys. Now, I have to get some sleep, if you don't mind."

Alexa turns back from the low windows to face Jimmy. "How many different places are there to fuel-up seaplanes around here?"

With his hands tucked behind his head, Jimmy lies on the pillow, thinking, and the thought begins to concern him. Alexa sits kindly on the edge of the bunk and alters her demeanor from demanding to charming.

"I know you need rest. Please, Jimmy, not here."

Jimmy takes a long look at her and sits up. He takes a deep breath and plants his feet on the floor. "Listen here… You're going to have to play it straight and level with me. What exactly is it they're after?"

The seaplane rocks gently in the water, as she stands and moves toward the hatch to look outside. "I can't tell you, but I will soon. For right now, we're in danger if we stay."

Jimmy glances over at his furry copilot in the corner, cheerfully grinning, oblivious to their dangerous situation. Bending low, he grabs up his leather boots to pull them on and starts with tying the laces. "We'll do it your way this time. I know an island not far from here where we'll be safe. I have to pay for the fuel, and then we'll take off."

Jimmy slides the fuel tally from his pocket and offers it to Alexa. She looks at him indifferently, and he rubs his fingertips together in reference to payment.

"This bird can't fly for free."

Alexa digs into the front of her bag and pulls out a wad of large bills. Peeling off three, she hands them over to Jimmy.

"How's cash?"

Her bank roll has him impressed, but his wonderment is interrupted by a quiet knocking near the port hatch door. They look over and see a stout little islander poking his head in from a small fishing boat bobbing alongside the seaplane. He smiles a chubby, sweat-glistened grin and eyes the interior of the cargo area. "Excuse me, Capt'n. You need ride to dock? You call me Chino. You want me to pay fuel bill for you?"

Alexa quickly tucks her money away and shakes off the startling surprise from the strange little man. Jimmy finishes lacing his boots and folds the fuel money into his pocket.

"Thanks, I'll take the ride."

"No problem, no problem. Chino take you."

Jimmy swings through the open hatch and steps into the small dinghy. The hairy copilot leaps from his perch in the corner and follows. Grabbing hold of Curtiss and placing him toward the bow, Jimmy looks back to Alexa at the seaplane doorway. "Be right back." He points a finger to the odd little man steering the boat. "Chino will take me."

She watches as the small boat putters away, zigzagging around the moored watercrafts toward the extended wooden pier and the village beyond. For a long moment, she takes another look around the crowded harbor. Feeling slightly relieved after not recognizing any of the boats or seaplanes, she ducks back inside.

Alexa sits back on the bunk and lays her head against the cool metal of the bulkhead. She closes her eyes briefly, sighs, and then lightly drifts off. The soft thud of something bumping against the moored seaplane hastily pulls her from the brief respite.

Alexa opens her eyes to the alarming sight of Chino staring at her. He stands in his boat, about waist high to the bottom of the open cargo hatch, and bobs slightly, up and down.

"You not from the islands?"

Unnerved by his stare, Alexa sits up and quickly gets her wits about her. "Uh, no. Just visiting."

"Where?"

"Where, what?"

"Where you visiting?"

"Um, Fiji."

The two are silent for an awkward moment. Chino's dark, beady eyes look out from round, sweaty cheeks and study Alexa intently. "Who you visiting?"

"Friends."

"Is the captain your friend?"

"Where is he?"

"He paying now."

Alexa looks out to the crowded harbor then back inside and around for an opportunity of a defensive weapon if needed.

"You sure have a lot of questions."

Chino continues to stare at her disconcertingly, as he sways in his boat outside the cargo access door. With the back of his hand, he wipes away the sweat that forms beneath the rolls under his chin and smiles a little, crooked-toothed grin.

"You have good visit, lady."

He looks over his right shoulder toward the wood pier, ducks from her view and then powers his little skiff away from the seaplane.

Alexa leaps to her feet and gapes out the open hatch, as Chino disappears around another larger sailboat. At the dock, she spots Jimmy catching another boat ride to the seaplane. She pulls herself back inside and paces the center aisle of the cargo area, trying to mull over the strange boatman's visit.

Alexa stands frozen in thought when, suddenly, she feels the small, hairy paws of Curtiss swing through her legs. The slight startle turns her to the cargo hatch, where she sees Jimmy peeking in and looking around.

"Alexa... Ready to go?"

She nods and swipes away the nervous sweat that glistens on her brow. The pilot climbs inside and notices her manner seems oddly peculiar. "You okay? What happened?"

"I'm fine. Let's get out of here."

Jimmy pulls the hatch door closed, fastens the latch, and turns to Alexa near the bulkhead. She smiles weakly, turning away to pet Curtiss in his corner nest. He watches her, concerned with the strange behavior, then moves to the front of the seaplane and slides behind the controls.

~*~

The Grumman seaplane idles clear of the mooring and taxies slowly across the crowded harbor. Along a dirt road, just outside the village, Chino scurries along, heading up into the jungled hills beyond. He looks out over the elevated view and watches as the blue-painted seaplane reaches open water. The engines roar, pulling the seaplane across turquoise water. White sprays of water shoot out from the hull, until the plane lifts up and launches into the clear afternoon sky.

Breathing hard, Chino mops his neck sweat with his hand again and turns up another dirt path toward a bamboo shack with a thatched roof. He bursts inside to a junk-cluttered room and moves to the overlooking window. Grabbing an extremely large pair of binoculars, he scans the sky and watches the seaplane until it fades into the distance.

Chino moves piles of assorted castoff items aside, and pulls a surplus military radio transmitter from under the table. He powers it up and waits while the machine hums, rattles and glows, bright with electricity. Still sweating, he breathes heavily into the dirt-covered radio transmitter. "Sea Dog One-Seven-Niner to Catalina P. M. R., do you copy?"

The radio breathes back only static while Chino pulls a filthy rag from his pocket and wipes the sweat forming at the tip of his nose. He runs the damp kerchief across his mouth, as he tries to control the panting in his breath. "Catalina P. M. R., this is Sea Dog One-Seven-Niner," he repeats.

The transmitter snaps back with an empty static, as he releases the button and raises the binoculars back to his face. The horizon is empty as the electronic device hums softly. Suddenly, there is a clicking sound on the radio receiver, and a faint voice materializes. "Copy that, this is Catalina P. M. R. ... Go ahead, Sea Dog One-Seven-Niner."

Putting the large binoculars on the side table, Chino raises the radio receiver to his mouth. His glistening cheeks peel back to reveal his tiny, crooked-teeth in a pudgy smile. Dabbing his face with the moist rag yet again, Chino breathes heavily into the electronic transmitter. "I have information of that woman and seaplane you seek. You can purchase, yes?"

Chino licks the perspiration from his upper lip, as he holds the radio receiver in his moist palm. The electronic unit hums a moment and then crackles to life.

"Standby, Sea Dog One-Seven-Niner."

Chapter 8

The white-and-blue Grumman seaplane flies across the clear, azure sky over an endless ocean that stretches in every direction. The large radial engines roar in sync with each other, as the props shimmer and spin like discs of glass. Seemingly static in the sparse clouds, the seaplane travels toward their next destination.

Jimmy is seated behind the controls, flying the seaplane as his eyelids and head grow heavy. Curtiss lies on the floor, curled in a ball on a crumpled coat between the captain chairs, snoring with a gentle purring sound. From the copilot's seat, Alexa takes notice of Jimmy drifting off behind the controls. She clears her throat loudly and adjusts her sunshade.

"How much longer till we get to this place?"

A bit startled, Jimmy blinks himself awake and makes adjustments to his flying. He jabs a finger toward her window. "That small group of clouds on the horizon, about one o'clock… Should be near there."

"You think it's safe?"

Jimmy glances over at her, tired and slightly irritated. "A friend of mine owns a tavern on the island. We can grab a bite to eat and catch some sleep. Nobody will find us there."

The sun glares through the front windshield, and Alexa pushes her sunglasses up on her nose. She eyes Jimmy and smiles with skeptical arrogance.

"Are you sure?"

Jimmy squints into the distance through the starboard window. A small group of islands can be seen faintly through the sparse clouds. He shakes his head and frowns at Alexa. "Yes, I'm sure. He's my friend." The airplane banks to the right, and the beams of sunlight shift across the cockpit as Jimmy steers toward the islands below.

Steadily approaching the isolated cluster of islands Jimmy adjusts the power on the overhead engine throttles. Alexa peers out the window at the large wooden lodge with a thin dock snaking out into the shallow surrounding waters. Jimmy circles the area once, looking over the two fishing boats and small, single-engine pontoon seaplane tied at the dock. He glances at Alexa and nods. "Suit you okay?"

"Do you know that airplane down there?"

Jimmy rolls his eyes and mutters sarcastically, as he slides open his port-side window. "It must be the noon rush... We should have made a reservation."

The expression on her face is not that of amusement, as she speaks loudly over the blowing rush of fresh air from the pilot-side window. "I'm talking about air pirates."

"If they are, only two fit in that puddle jumper."

Alexa studies the palm-log and thatched-roof building. Pink shells are arranged on the roof to spell out the name of the tavern: CUTTER'S PLACE.

She observes the rambling structure along the wide, sandy beach and shrugs her approval. Curtiss sits up and leaps to her lap, peering out the window at the island below. Jimmy grins like a young boy hiding a childish secret, as he adjusts the throttles and banks the seaplane in for a landing.

Flying low across crystal-clear waters, the seaplane roars over the surface and gently touches down with a spray of water diverted off the hull. Jimmy taxies the seaplane past the long, meandering dock and steers toward the adjacent stretch of beach.

Hints of sea-spray mist through the open port window, while Alexa watches a grinning Jimmy, pull off his headset. She peers at him over the top of her brown-tinted sunglasses. "So... We're going to Cutter's Place?"

"Yup. It's good to be back."

The boat-plane rumbles toward the sandy shoreline. Jimmy pulls a lever that lowers the amphibious wheels from the side of the airframe into the water. Slowly, the seaplane rolls itself out of the surf and eases up onto the empty beach. The right engine roars as the plane pivots on the opposite braked wheel, turning out to face the ocean horizon again. Water trickles from the vacant wheel hulls, as the shut-off engines whirl the props to a standstill.

When the rear-access cargo hatch opens, Curtiss leaps out and rolls onto the sandy beach. In disbelief,

Alexa peers around at the hulking structure of the remote island tavern. She turns to Jimmy as he grabs his duffle. "What is this place? It looks like a hideout for Peter Pan and the Lost Boys."

Jimmy smiles and checks the ammo clip on his gun. "You won't find any Tinkerbells or fairies here."

Watching Jimmy inspect his handgun, Alexa stands before him questioningly. "I thought you said he was your friend?"

He looks down at the slab-sided 1911 auto pistol, shrugs, and tucks it in his back waistband. "Yeah... So?"

"You're quite the Boy Scout."

"With friends like mine, you have to be prepared for anything."

"Prepared for what exactly?"

The beach is hard-packed sand littered with tree fronds and washings from the dropping tide. Jimmy helps Alexa from the rear hatch to the beach and tosses his bag next to her. Ignoring his duffle, she takes the furry copilot's hand and walks the palm-littered beach toward the tavern.

Jimmy jumps down to the gray sand and runs his hand over the wet, dripping body of the seaplane. He gives his prized water-bird a quick once-over and frowns at the fresh bullet holes plinked laterally behind the left window. Grabbing up the bag, he watches Curtiss walking devotedly alongside Alexa and follows.

~*~

Inside the high-beam roofed tavern, it is cool and dark with natural light coming in only through the front windows. Wooden tables and chairs are crammed to the side of the room near a bamboo-constructed bar set before a dirty edge-flacked mirror. Snapshots and framed photos of old airplanes, boats, and war memorabilia fill the walls and clutter the bar-back.

A silhouetted figure stands near the window and watches the new arrivals coming from the beach. The looming figure takes a drag from a short, thick cigar, exhales slowly, and then tosses it away. The smoky haze hangs in the streaming sunlight and languidly whirls, as the broad form moves from sight.

~*~

At the edge of the strand, next to the stilted lodge structure, Alexa waits with Curtiss and gracefully ushers Jimmy forward. "After you, Captain." The sandy beach gives way to crushed coral as Jimmy marches on. He gives her a humored smile and proceeds up a log-planked incline that connects with the boat dock.

Jimmy pauses on the front porch of the tavern and peers through the opened doorway into the dimly lit interior. A chair creaks and tips back on two legs away from the light, concealing the watching occupant. The long, cutting shadows cover all but the lumberjack-styled boots lifted off the floor.

At the threshold to the tavern, Jimmy waits to let his eyes adjust to the low light. He counts three men at the bar: two fishermen and another he recognizes as a seaplane pilot named Archie. The men, not expecting any casual visitors, turn to the obscure figure backlit in the doorway.

Jimmy glances over his shoulder at Alexa and Curtiss still coming up the ramp from the beach, and then back inside toward the bar. He hollers across the room to the scrawny seaplane pilot sitting at the end of the bar. "Hey, Archie. Where's Cutter?" Instantly, a knife slices through the air and sticks in the doorjamb a few inches from Jimmy's head. Jimmy quickly pulls his pistol and snaps off a shot into the shadows.

The man tilts forward in the chair, letting the sunlight catch his rough, leathery features. Jimmy lowers the smoking handgun and looks to the ray of sunlight shining through the bullet hole in the wall at the spot where the man's head was. A friendly smirk starts to appear at the corner of Jimmy's mouth, as he speaks to the shadowed figure. "Hello, Cutter." Jimmy turns to the knife sticking in the jamb near his face. "Looks like we're both a little rusty."

The broken light accents Cutter as he smiles like a storybook sea pirate. He shrugs his large shoulders and adjusts his loose linen shirt over his bulging torso. "Hell, Jim, you're not even worth getting my knife dirty."

Cutter leans over and glances out the window at the glistening white-and-blue, high-winged seaplane on the sandy beach. "Thought that sounded like yer bird. How's she flying?"

"Good as ever, 'nd still not for sale."

With a roaring laugh, Cutter rocks forward in his chair. "What brings you to these waters?"

There is an interrupting cough and Alexa steps through the doorway with Curtiss. Jimmy moves aside and gives a mock salute toward Cutter. "I'm playing island tour guide."

Skeptical of the situation, Alexa watches Jimmy tuck his gun away before looking to the large bowie knife stuck in the doorjamb. "Am I interrupting you two killing each other?"

Cutter stands and lets the chair drop to the floor, kicks it aside, and then strolls over toward Alexa. He stops uncomfortably near to her, reaches out, and unsticks his knife from the jamb with a heavy jerk before calmly sheathing it.

"Nope. Not much of a contest."

His tobacco-tinged breath sweeps Alexa's senses in an odd mix of danger and mystery. She steps inside, past Cutter. The coolness of the room is an inviting retreat from the midday sun. Cutter smiles broadly at Jimmy, then back to Alexa as he touches her under the chin. His dark eyes peer into hers. "The name's Cutter. Whom do I have the pleasure of having as my special lady guest?"

Alexa holds her ground and takes Cutter's hand from her face. "Alexa Reid."

Cutter's left eyebrow rises up. "The famed archaeologist and treasure hunter?"

Surprised, Jimmy notices Cutter eagerly size-up the lady traveler when he recognizes her name. The seaplane pilot takes a step forward and pats the tavern owner on the shoulder. "You betcha. The one and only."

Following the monkey copilot's lead, Jimmy walks to the bar and nods to the men observing from the other end of the hardwood slab. Jimmy notices their eyes suspiciously divert away, as he slaps his hand on the bar.

"Now that everyone has met, ya think we could get something to drink and eat?"

He lifts Curtiss to one of the barstools and turns, as Archie quickly finishes his drink and gets up to leave.

"Where you off to, Archie?"

"Nowhere. Just stuff to do, places to be."

"You been keeping busy?"

"Yeah, yeah… Kinda."

The shifty-eyed pilot nervously tosses a few crumpled bills on the bar top. Jimmy and Curtiss watch Archie fake a feeble smile, turn, and scurry outside to the seaplane dock. They watch him descend the stairs until he is out of sight, and Jimmy exchanges a humorous grimace with his furry copilot. The fishermen murmur to each other under their breath, then grudgingly move their drinks to an adjacent table with chairs.

Making a show of it, Cutter escorts Alexa across the room and, acting the gentleman, offers her a stool. He steps behind the bar, leans down on the wood slab with his brawny forearms and yells over his shoulder toward the kitchen. "Hey, Manny!"

A round, dark-skinned native man steps out of the kitchen and smiles. He acknowledges Jimmy and Curtiss with a friendly salute. Cutter grabs a ceramic jug of homemade liquor and gives the concoction a shake. "Manny, go ahead and cook up some plates of food for our good friend Curtiss, his chauffeur, and their guest."

Manny ducks back into the kitchen and Cutter grabs up four stout cocktail glasses. He laughs, as he sees Curtiss rub his furry fingers together and lick his lips with anticipation.

"What do ya say, four Mad-Moondogs?"

Alexa shakes her head while he generously pours the four shots of alcohol. "I think I'll pass on the drink,"

"Nonsense. It's on the house. Jimmy here used to drink these like water."

Rubbing the palm of his hand under his unshaven chin, Jimmy shakes his head and smirks.

"I wouldn't recommend it."

With a generous smile, Cutter passes the drinks around and Curtiss immediately dips a pointed finger in his glass. Cutter nods, pleased, and winks at Jimmy, "I see he still has your manners. Down the hatch. "He lifts his glass, downs it, and Jimmy follows his lead.

Alexa smells the drink cautiously at first, then lifts it to her pursed lips, tips it back, and releases it down her throat. Cutter watches, delighted, as she gives a cough and a shiver.

With a sweep of his burly arm, Cutter gathers up the empty glasses and begins pouring from the jug again. "Another round?"

"I'll just take a soda... How about a soda-pop over here for the Captain, too. He still has to fly me around today."

Exchanging a sly look with Jimmy, Cutter smiles and continues pouring the drinks. "Bossy, ain't she?"

Cutter slides Jimmy another drink and Alexa grabs it midway and slides it back. Easing back on his stool, Jimmy seems to enjoy the sudden confrontation between the two. Alexa stares dead-on with Cutter who has developed an insulted scowl. She tries to disarm him with a quaint smile.

"No, thanks."

The friendly tavern owner's features turn ominous. "You refuse my hospitality?"

"I am paying for a tour, not a drunken pilot."

Jimmy leans forward, about to interject, and Alexa shoots him a cold stare that stops him short.

With both large mitts planted on the bar, his sausage fingers tapping a measured beat, Cutter leans in closer to Alexa, nearly growling. "When I offer a drink, it gets drunk."

Alexa locks eyes with the vexed bartender and reaches out for Jimmy's shot of mysterious liquor. She takes the mixture and pours it into her own glass, making it a double. Still locked in his gaze, Alexa raises her full tumbler and gives Cutter a nod.

"Cheers."

Cutter cracks a crooked smile and raises his own glass. "I like your style, Ms. Reid."

They both tip back the drinks and let the alcohol burn its way down. Cutter smiles, as he watches Alexa grip the bar while letting the mixture settle in. She wipes her lips and slides the glass aside, which clinks with Curtiss's drink.

"Now, soda pops please, for me and the captain."

Jimmy grins as Cutter looks to him approvingly, and they exchange amused expressions.

Chapter 9

Seated at a table, having enjoyed a feast of a meal, Jimmy sits back with empty plates before him and a half-finished soda. Curtiss lies nearby, napping and sunning himself on the window sill. Alexa scoots her chair from the table, stands, and runs her palm across her middle.

"Excuse me. I have to use the powder room."

Jimmy waves her off toward the facilities and takes another swig from the recycled soda bottle. He rolls the end of the scuffed glass on the rough-hewn table and stares outside.

Coming from the kitchen, Cutter watches Alexa's exit. He walks over to Jimmy and pulls up a chair alongside him. His friendly demeanor has changed, and he's oddly serious.

"Why are you here, Jimmy?"

Jimmy pushes back and looks at his pal strangely. "Just came for some food and friendly service."

"What's the deal with the broad?"

"No deal. Just showing her around."

Cutter eyes Jimmy suspiciously. He stands and stacks a few dirty plates. Forks clang on the empty dishware and his arching brow lifts questioningly.

"You sure that's all?" Cutter continues to pile the plates and lifts them from the table. "How long you staying, Jim?"

Leaning back in his chair, Jimmy seems surprised by the question. "You want to get rid of me? I haven't been by in a while, and figured I'd take advantage of your hospitality... maybe catch a nap. Why the rush and early checkout?"

"No reason, just curious. Of course, you're welcome to the cots on the back porch."

"Thanks."

Cutter looks over as Alexa steps out of the bathroom. He smiles at her, as he takes the load of dishes to the kitchen. The wooden chair rumbles, as it's dragged across the plank floor when Alexa takes her seat. She notices Jimmy is unusually quiet and rubbing his eyes. "What's up?"

"Nothing. Just tired."

He stares out the front window toward the lone pontoon seaplane still tied on the dock near the fishing boats. "Hmm, Archie is still here? I thought he left."

Drowsy and looking worn-out, Jimmy lets his gaze travel around the empty room. "I need some sleep."

Alexa observes the napping monkey in the window box and the exhausted pilot seated across the table from her. She looks around the vacant surroundings and nods in agreement. "Alright, just an hour or two... Then we are out of here."

"Fine." Jimmy grabs up his soda bottle and tips back the last swallow.

~*~

The sound of heavy breathing comes from one of the cots in the back room. Jimmy sleeps peacefully, as Alexa stares up at the wood-hewn plank ceiling and bug-screen windows. She turns over and watches as the door to the tavern silently opens a crack. The sleepy form of Curtiss ambles in and then climbs into a patio chair to continue his nap.

As the door swings gently closed, Alexa hears several voices talking quietly outside. She gets up, goes to the partially opened door, peers out, and listens. Out in the lodge's main room, Alexa can see Archie and the two fishermen talking with Cutter at the bar. A '97 sawed-off pump-shotgun is laid out across the bar with another pistol visible in Archie's waistband. Cutter shakes his head, seemingly reluctant to what the others have to say.

One of the fishermen draws his gun and, in an instant, Cutter has his knife blade out, and under the man's chin. Archie quickly motions for a peaceful calm. He glances over his shoulder at the back room, and Alexa ducks away as the weapons are tucked away momentarily. The scrawny seaplane pilot leans in close to the bar and whispers something in Cutter's ear.

The two continue a heated debate, with whispered voices, until Cutter glances at the sleeping porch and pauses. He stands behind the bar and looks back at the two fishermen, then turns his stern gaze on Archie. Alexa watches as Cutter steals another glimpse toward the back porch, and then gives a hesitant nod of agreement. She quickly ducks back from the door and quietly moves to where Jimmy is still sound asleep on the wood-framed cot. With a gentle shake, she whispers loudly in his ear. "Jimmy... Jimmy, wake up!"

Stirring, Jimmy rolls over with an annoyed moan. "Yeah, yeah baby..."

Alexa tightly cups her hand over his mouth and delivers a solid punch to his arm. His eyes suddenly dart open wide with surprise. A moan escapes from under her palm as he holds his tender arm. His gaze rolls to her hand on his mouth and up to her questioningly.

She looms over him with a look of hard determination and seems grimly serious. Alexa bends down to Jimmy on the low cot and whispers urgently. "We have to get out of here now. Get up... Your friends are about to turn on you."

He stares up at her, bewildered, as she releases her cupped hand from over his mouth. Coming out of a satiating slumber, he sputters, "Woman, have you gone totally nuts?! What are you talking about?"

"I can't explain it to you now. They've talked it over already and will be coming for us in a minute."

Jimmy sits up and wipes the sleep from his eyes. "Who's been talking?"

"Your friends!"

"Cutter?"

"And the other three."

"What?"

"Your pal Archie and his fishing boat cronies."

The realization of what she is saying suddenly sinks in. Snapping to action, Jimmy grabs his pistol from inside one of the boots on the floor and quickly pulls them on. He looks over at Curtiss still sleeping in the chair, and then up at Alexa.

"Wake him up."

~*~

In the main room of the lodge, the two fishermen creep toward the back porch door with pistols raised. Archie follows behind with the shotgun held across his chest, at the ready. Slowly, they nudge the door ajar and peek out to the screened, sleeping area. Archie looks past his two associates and sees that all the beds are empty. "What the hell? Where'd they go?"

The three step into the empty room and scan it from floor to ceiling. The fishermen press their faces to the mesh windows and look to the jungle tree fronds and water below. Hearing a discontented grunt at the doorway, Archie turns to see Cutter remove a chomped cigar stub from between his teeth, spit, and shake his head knowingly.

The ambush-scheming pilot, Archie, lowers his shotgun and whines. "What's the deal, Cutter? Where did they go?" Cutter strides to the end of the room and pushes one of the cots aside with the toe of his boot. He kneels and puts his finger through a hole in the floor, pulling up a secret hatch. Archie's jaw drops and he looks at Cutter dismayed.

"What the heck is that?"

The brawny owner of the lodge looks down at the collection of footprints in the sandy ground below and turns angrily to Archie. "I thought they didn't know what you were up to, you sneaky bastard!" He slams the wooden floor hatch down and stands. "They're probably to the plane by now. Your big money reward is about to take wing 'nd fly away."

Without a second thought, the two fishermen run out the doorway through the lodge, followed closely by Archie. The three men dash across the vacant tavern, hurrying to get outside, in an attempt to intercept the plane before it takes off. The first man to the front entry is met by an angry fist to the face from outside the door. He stumbles back, holding his nose. The other fisherman runs into the first, and they trip over themselves.

Jimmy pokes his head into the entryway to see Archie stop mid-room with the pump shotgun in hand. Their eyes connect for a split second before Archie develops a distinct look of panic. He raises the shotgun, aiming toward Jimmy at the door, while the fishermen roll away to cover. Jimmy ducks back as the shotgun lets loose, turning half the doorframe to splinters.

The air is calm a moment, as slivers of wood drop to the floor and a burnt gunpowder haze hangs in a cloud of smoke. Jimmy leaps through the open window while firing his automatic pistol at Archie. Several shots tear up the wall behind the bar, and one hits the scrawny pilot in the shoulder. With a yelp, Archie drops the shotgun, and it rattles to the floor. From the sleeping porch, Cutter watches as Archie holds his wounded shoulder and flees to cover, leaving the scattergun in the center of the room.

As gunshots are fired from the two fishermen, Jimmy overturns a stout hardwood table and hunkers down behind it, firing off several rounds in return. Bullet-lead and splinters of smashed wood explode through the rough-hewn surface. Jimmy ducks and pops up again at the far edge of the table, snapping off several shots. One of the fishermen takes a hit to the chest and tumbles back over a stack of wooden chairs.

During a lull in the gunfire, Jimmy peeks around the table to see Cutter looking out from the rear sleeping porch. The tavern owner smiles at Jimmy and, in a blink of an eye, Cutter's knife whirls through the air and sticks in the table just an inch below its intended target. Startled, Jimmy glances down at the deadly knife, as Cutter darts out into the room.

The floorboards pound as if there was a bull charging through the tavern, as Cutter thunders toward the abandoned shotgun left on the floor. He covers the short distance quickly, the other assailants watching and waiting to see the outcome. As Cutter swoops down to grab hold of the idle weapon, Jimmy lunges from concealed cover and tackles him, knocking him into the surrounding tables and chairs.

In quick succession, Jimmy lands several solid punches on the larger opponent. Unfazed, Cutter regains his footing, grabs hold of Jimmy, and tosses him across the room into the bamboo-trimmed bar. The solid piece of furniture deflects Jimmy to the floor, and Cutter strolls up to loom over him.

"This ain't gonna be pretty, pal..."

Cutter flashes a grin, only to receive a kick directly to his knee that crumples him to the floor.

Eye-to-eye on the floor, Jimmy faces off with his old, wartime buddy. They glare at each other a telling moment, before Cutter gives a knowing smirk to an answering shrug. They lash out simultaneously. Jimmy connects a roundhouse punch to Cutter's temple, as Cutter returns a thrusting punch into Jimmy's gut.

Cutter's eye blinks at the cracking impact of knuckles and grabs Jimmy by the ankle. He climbs to his feet and swings Jimmy around the room twice, crashing him into furniture before letting him fly through the legs of a table. Both men return to their feet and resume throwing punches. They tear viciously at each other, turning the room inside out.

Exchanging several extended rounds of violent blows, Jimmy and Cutter smash each other around the room and eventually drop to the floor in fatigue. Suddenly a shotgun blast startles them to attention and brings the battle to an end. They gawk skyward through the wreckage, to a gaping hole in the thatched roof and over to Alexa holding the sawed-off shotgun. She gives the smoking gun a violent pump and unloads another round of buckshot at the bar.

On his knees next to Jimmy, Cutter cringes at the shattered liquor bottles and the damage to the bamboo ceiling. He mourns the destruction and the loss of alcohol, moaning, "What the hell was that for?"

One-handed, Alexa gives the shotgun another pump. The ejected twelve-gauge brass shell casing clanks to the floor and she looks around the gunpowder-hazed and compliantly hushed room. "I wanted to be sure to have your attention."

She turns her stare to Jimmy, as he rises to his haunches and touches the source of blood over his eye.

"Jimmy, you okay?"

"Yeah…"

There is a scuffling movement coming from the corner, and Archie yells out, "Shoot them, damn you!"

Quickly turning and letting loose with the shotgun, Alexa blasts the armed fishermen back against the rear wall. His gun drops to the floor, as he slumps down in a dead heap. Cutter whistles through a bloody, swollen lip.

"Cripe…"

Jimmy slowly climbs to his feet and grabs up his pistol from the floor. He looks over at Cutter, seated on the thatch-littered floorboards with Alexa standing over him, shotgun at the ready. The pair watch, as Jimmy walks over toward the wall and kicks a table out of the way. The table crashes into several chairs and reveals Archie cowering on the floor, holding the sleeve of his bleeding shoulder.

Jimmy points his gun at Archie and glares down at the quivering man. "Archie, old pal. What's doin'?"

"How do you mean?"

Looking around the thrashed barroom, Jimmy puts a boot heel to Archie's fresh bullet wound, pinning him back against the wall. "Archie, explain please."

Archie cries in pain, as Jimmy gives his heel a twist. "Wait, Jimmy! I thought we were friends…"

"Wrong."

The scrawny man writhes in agony as Jimmy applies more pressure in his interrogation. "Why the ambush, Arch?"

"There's a hefty bounty out on you two!"

Jimmy gazes inquisitively to Alexa and back to Archie. The wounded man takes a deep breath, as Jimmy removes the sole of his boot from his injured shoulder. Archie sits up and shrugs sheepishly. "They want her mostly alive, and you..." He slices a single finger across his neckline and smiles apologetically. Jimmy pauses a moment and lowers his gun.

"Who?"

From behind in the barroom, Cutter begins to laugh. Jimmy turns to look at him and Alexa.

Cutter spits a gob of blood to the side and wipes the back of his hand across his mouth. He sits cross-legged on the floor, leans back on one hand, and smiles at Jimmy. "Who do you think?" Jimmy growls at Cutter, "Why don't you tell me?"

"It is all over the air waves. Rasmus and his pirates have turned you and this treasure dame into the biggest trophy since Captain Kidd sailed these waters."

Jimmy aims his pistol directly at Cutter and gestures to him with the pointed firearm. "What part do you have in this? I never thought you to be a flunky for pirates."

"Jimmy, you have to understand."

"Understand what? We've been through a lot together. Hell, I'm your friend!"

Cutter sits upright and brushes his big hands together, smiling at Jimmy. "Well, the thing is, you ain't worth so much. But her, we're talking a *lot* of money."

Archie eases himself from the wall and leans toward Jimmy to whisper loudly, "Yes, yes, a whole lot of money. You want in on a cut?"

Jimmy turns and pistol whips Archie across the face, dropping him to the floor in a pile. He aims his gun back at Cutter and shakes his head disappointed.

"You haven't changed."

"Nor have you. Still with that badge of honor pinned to yer chest while passing up the easy money."

Jimmy moves across the room and looks outside at the two sailing vessels and the small seaplane secured at the dock. A slight breeze clears the gun smoke from the room, and he turns, looking toward Cutter still seated on the floor.

"Anyone else out there?"

"Nope, you've wasted all my customers."

Jimmy's gaze connects with Alexa, with the loaded shotgun, still standing over Cutter. He tilts his head over to the doorway, and she starts to back toward it. He waits for her to step outside and glares down at Cutter. "We're leaving. You going to try to stop us?"

"Didn't feel right about it anyway."

Cutter climbs to his feet and ushers Jimmy to the exit. He rubs his bearded jaw and smears blood from his nose into his moustache. "It's a damn shame someone else is going to get all that reward money though."

"I wouldn't lose any sleep over it."

Cutter follows Jimmy to the front of the tavern and pulls his knife blade from the wooden table as he passes. Jimmy stops just outside the entrance and pauses, as Curtiss comes from behind a dock pylon and wraps his arms around his partner's leg. Jimmy gives the monkey an affectionate pat on the head and pulls him free, handing him over to Alexa.

"Take Curtiss to the plane."

Both men watch as Alexa and Curtiss run down the wood-and-rope fashioned ramp to the beach and the waiting amphibious seaplane. Cutter takes a step forward and adjusts his grip on the bone-handled knife, concealed behind his back. "Jim, I don't think you understand what you got yourself into. Her uncle and his band of pirates got more pull 'round here than ya think. This won't stop 'til they get their hooks in you. Your best chance is to jest be rid of 'er."

A look of surprise shows fleetingly on Jimmy's face and, amused, Cutter laughs. "Didn't know they were related? I'll bet you don't know the half of what you've got yourself set up for with this dame. You remember the stories of Rasmus, heard during the war? Well, a lot of 'em is true, 'nd then some. She is all trouble wrapped up in a pretty lookin' package."

Cutter readies his knife and slowly brings it around. Jimmy takes a step away, raises his gun, and points it at his old friend. "Make a move, and I won't regret shooting you."

Cutter smiles a wolfish grin and lets the knife blade fall with a thud, sticking into the floor at his heels.

"Wouldn't blame you, ol' buddy."

"Sorry I don't have time to settle my bar tab."

"What's new?"

Jimmy steps down the ramp to the waiting seaplane. He keeps the aim of his gun trained on his smiling associate. As Jimmy reaches the beach, Cutter gives him a saluting wave and shouts, "Good luck, Jim. No hard feelings?"

"Sure... Thanks!"

Jimmy turns and jogs the short distance to the parked seaplane. He climbs inside the cargo hatch and closes the door behind him. Gentle waves lap under the dock, as Cutter strolls down the length of the wooden structure to watch as the flying boat's engines whine, then growl to life. He waves again when he sees Jimmy glance over at him through the sliding port window.

"Good luck, pal... You'll need it."

The engines throttle up to a roar and the high-winged seaplane rolls forward to the water before the wheels retract into the floating body. The whirling propellers and the spray from the stepped-hull leave a churned path through the bay as the flying boat leaps into the air, leaving a mist of clinging water in its wake.

At the end of the dock, Cutter leans on one of the wood pilings and takes a broken cigar from his upper breast pocket. Thick fingers snap the loose bits of tobacco leaves away, scattering them to the breeze. He clenches the remaining stub between his teeth and watches, as the distinct sound and silhouette of the seaplane disappear into the afternoon sky.

Chapter 10

The roar and vibration of the twin radial Pratt & Whitney engines tickle Alexa's ears, as Jimmy flies the seaplane while she sits quietly in the copilot chair. The fresh blood is mostly cleaned from his face, revealing several swollen cuts and bruises that serve as souvenirs of the scuffle. He looks at her and adjusts his headset. "Sorry about the situation back there. I had no idea how bad that Rasmus character wanted you."

"I'm sorry about your friends."

"They weren't all my friends." Jimmy gives her a telling, sidelong glance. "Anyone who'd lie to you can't be trusted anyway." He turns back to watching the horizon, as Alexa sits in awkward silence. The drone of the twin engines rumble in place of any conversation.

~*~

Adjusting the aircraft's navigational instruments, Jimmy references the coordinates on the slip of paper again. He checks his timepiece and then peers down to the map of the islands on his lap. Alexa emerges from the cargo area and sits in the copilot chair again. Through the starboard window, she watches the water below, then turns to Jimmy and smiles inquiringly.

"When do you think we will get there?"

He starts to turn his head toward her but then stops, wincing from one of the knuckle-induced gashes near his eye. "We have to make another stop."

"What kind of a stop?"

"A friend has an island an hour from here."

The furry copilot's long tail curls up between Jimmy and Alexa, and brushes along the side of the captain's chair. Jimmy reaches down to pet Curtiss. The monkey puts a foot on each chair seat and lifts himself up in a straddled position to look out the front windshield. He lays one of his small hands on Alexa's shoulder as she scratches his belly.

She peers around the monkey to the pilot and smirks. "No offense, but this is the only friend of yours that I like so far." She smooths her hand down the back of the copilot and eyes Jimmy. "Can you trust this guy?"

Jimmy grimaces over toward Curtiss and then Alexa. "Well, he doesn't have any use for money or own a wireless." He grins to himself, satisfied, and banks the plane to the west.

The radial engines thunder in sync as the white-and-blue flying boat soars across clear sky, over an ocean that stretches endlessly in every direction. The seaplane glistens and shimmers as it flies into the afternoon sky, nearing the remote island destination.

~*~

An hour later, the seaplane buzzes over a grouping of small islands that appear to be mostly uninhabited. The high-winged boat-plane flies low over the largest landmass, and they soon sight a single T-shaped dock extending several meters out into the water on the windward side. On the dock, three quarters of the length out, sits a wooden sailing sloop, fastened loosely, in the calm, aquamarine waters of the South Pacific.

The airplane comes around and makes a second pass. Jimmy rocks his wings over the island and flies closer to the dock, as a man walks out and waves a welcome gesture. Jimmy tips his wing in response and flies past. He banks the flying boat again and approaches for a sea landing.

Jimmy prepares to touch down on the water, and Alexa holds Curtiss to her lap. She moves his head aside and looks to Jimmy. "How well do you know this guy?"

Jimmy looks up from his instruments. "Who... Quint?" He stifles a laugh when he notices Alexa's concerned look. "Well, enough not to trust him. I'm just kidding... He's fine. He was a pro at running supplies and doing some smalltime smuggling during the war."

"Sounds like an upright citizen."

"Just wait until you meet him." Jimmy raises his eyebrows and smirks.

In a cresting spray of surf, the Grumman seaplane touches down and taxies across the crystal clear waters. Jimmy reaches up and reduces the engine power, as they near the T-shaped end of the wooden pier. The lean figure of an amused Quint Laffite can be seen waiting on the dock.

A mature man, appearing to be in his middle sixties, Quint has shoulder-length silver hair and a dark tan that highlights the large amount of chest hair on his shirtless torso. With the ease and grace of a young athlete, Quint mentally gauges the seaplane's approach and gives the starboard wingtip a push skyward, providing the wing pontoon and engine propeller extra clearance over the low wooden dock.

Alexa looks out the sun-glared window and watches the bare-footed expat nimbly toss a rope around the cleat of the seaplane and lash it down with the skill of an old sailor. His messy hair hangs down as he works, and she quickly looks away when he tosses his mop of tresses back to peer, with a pearly-toothed grin, into the aircraft cabin. This rugged and virile being is inescapably compelling to Alexa, stirring her curiosity. "How old is this Quint?"

Jimmy finishes shutting everything down, pulls his headphones off, and sets them aside. He glances out the window at Quint and waves. "I have no idea. Why?"

"He looks wild."

Jimmy smiles, as he ducks down and crawls into the nose compartment. "He is wild..."

Curtiss jumps to the floor and follows Jimmy, as Alexa peeks out the window to observe their island host.

The engines hiss and tick with the heat of exhaust, as the front nose hatch opens and Jimmy pokes his head out. Quint puts his hands to his hips and smiles welcomingly.

"What brings you to these parts, Jimmy?"

Jimmy secures the loop of the tie-down rope over the nose cleat and tosses the rest of the coil to Quint, who squats to fasten it on the dock.

"Just checking in on you to make sure you're keeping out of trouble in this corner of the world."

Quint looks up from his squatted position and narrows an eye skeptically, peering through the windows of the floating seaplane. "It appears that you're the one who needs keeping out of trouble. I see you have a woman along."

Jimmy slides out of the hatch and hops to the dock. Curtiss stands on the nose of the flying boat and immediately leaps into Quint's arms. The weathered islander holds the hairy monkey, copilot in his arms and greets him warmly. "How ya doin', Curtiss? I think I have some of your special island rum inside." Quint lets Curtiss leap to the dock and curiously watches as Jimmy walks the length of his seaplane, inspecting it.

The old sailor changes his focus when Alexa emerges from the nose hatch and looks around. Quint's eyes light up at the sight of her youthful beauty. "Jimmy... Never mind about your floating water scooter. I don't think you've introduced me to this lovely lady."

Passing his fingers under the wing, Jimmy walks back to Quint. "*Quintcannon Laffite*, meet Alexa Reid... The reason I'm this far down on the backside of the world..."

"You can call me Quint. I am at your service."

Quint bows slightly before offering his hand to help her to the dock from the forward nose hatch. Alexa smiles, overwhelmed by his primitive, masculine charm.

"Thank you, Quint."

He gives her a sensual smile and a kiss on the hand, which makes her insides tingle and nearly melt with emotion. He looks up from her hand to meet her gaze, and his eyes sparkle with a remarkable virility, despite his age.

"To what do I owe this visit?"

Mouth agape, Alexa is about to speak as Jimmy steps between them and interjects. "She's on an expedition to look at the islands around these parts."

Alexa moves around Jimmy and stands closer to Quint. "I'm doing mostly research on the island's history of inhabitance and the prevailing traditions and lore."

With a keen eye for the details, Quint studies Alexa. "The story of these islands can be summed up very easily. These islands were only frequented by cannibals and pirates. There's been no proper civilization to speak of."

Jimmy rolls his eyes. "It seems not much has changed. That is about all I've shown her so far."

Alexa brushes Jimmy off with a kind smile while keeping her attention on Quint. "I'd like to see it for myself... and experience it."

Quint puts her soft palm in his, and she feels the firm grasp of his callused, hardworking hands. The older, gentleman places his arm around her and smiles warmly. "Yes, I guess you will. Let me show you my home. It's a work in progress, but the most civilization you'll see in these parts."

As they begin to walk down the length of dock, she stops and separates herself from Quint. "Will you excuse me a minute?"

Alexa walks back to Jimmy, as he holds one of the propeller props and peers into the steaming engine cowling. "Captain Ferral, what about the airplane?"

"Workin' fine, thanks."

"No, wouldn't it be a good idea to hide it?"

Jimmy wipes his hands on his khaki shorts and looks down the length of the floating seaplane. Turning to look over his shoulder, Jimmy faces out to the wide expanse of vast unoccupied seascape. He gestures sarcastically around him at the open horizon. "It's hidden. No one comes near to here."

"*They* will."

Jimmy rubs his tired face in surrender and calls out to Quint, who waits farther down the dock. "Quint, do you mind if I use the beach under the trees? I have some work to do."

"Sure thing. Do you need some help?"

The tired pilot smiles tersely at Alexa and then looks back at Quint. "Yes. Take her away, so she'll leave me alone, and I'll have peace for an hour or two."

Alexa stands uncomfortably, as Quint grins eagerly. Jimmy walks away along the boarded walkway, murmuring aloud as he unties the dock lines. "If you happen to lose her on the island somewhere, it would be a great favor to me."

She listens to Jimmy and gives an exasperated huff. "Real nice, Captain Ferral..."

Alexa scans the concealing shelter of the vegetation along the beach landing and loudly whispers toward Jimmy. "Don't you worry... I'll be sure to leave you alone with your beloved winged-boat. Just make sure you hide it from view." Annoyed, Jimmy glances at her, as she goes to rejoin Quint.

She takes his offered arm and, with Curtiss in tow, saunters up the dock. The man, woman and monkey step from the marina to the shore and, without looking back, disappear on a path through the leafy palms and underbrush. Jimmy watches for a lingering moment before climbing inside the seaplane's nose hatch and pulling it closed behind him with a solid slam.

Chapter 11

At the edge of the beach landing, under bushy, untrimmed palm trees and dense jungle-foliage, the parked seaplane looks the romantic picture of paradise. The sporadic chatter of birds and exotic insects, overlays the soft, rhythmic lap of waves on the beach that suggests the gentle heartbeat of the island. Jimmy lies stretched out in a hammock, slung between the extended wheel strut and the wingtip pontoon float.

The quiet patter of footsteps walking down the jungle path from the house causes Jimmy to stir and roll to his side. Sand cascades off the shoeless feet that step around fallen palm fronds. The island resident, Quint, walks the beach and approaches the plane. He observes Jimmy, seemingly in the act of slumber, and circles the amphibious flying-machine with a curious eye.

The seaplane fuselage, perched high on its wheels, appears larger when raised out from the level of the water. Jimmy sits up to a lounging position in the hammock and opens an eye toward the visitor.

"What are you looking for, Quint?"

Interrupted in his inspection, he turns to Jimmy. "That's funny, I was going to ask you the same thing."

Putting hands above his head to rub his hair, Jimmy groans. He swings a leg over the side of the slung canvas cradle and gives a slight push. "Why's that?"

Quint takes a seat on a piece of driftwood at the edge of the clearing and digs his toes deep in the sand. "Well, I was having a conversation with that gal of yours." The islander buries his feet in the cool sand, which fills between his defined arches, and he brushes his hair back behind his ears. "I find it interesting, for someone who has been researching these islands, that she doesn't really know squat." Quint grins knowingly. "She pretends pretty well and talks a good game, but it don't amount to much." The long-haired island sage picks up a crooked stick and scratches his back through his loosely draped linen shirt. He gazes over at Jimmy in the hammock and continues, "Which is just fine, except, after talking with her more, she does know a whole lot about many other things. It got me thinking that she may have other interests."

Jimmy tries to act casual while scratching his head and gazing over at Quint. "She just arrived out here in the islands. I only met her a day or two ago."

Quint tosses the stick away and puts his hands to his knees. He stares at Jimmy for a deliberate moment and then nods. "Yeah, that's what I figured at first. But then, I remembered where I've heard her name."

Jimmy gets the uneasy feeling of being on the short end of the facts again. He thinks back to what Cutter said about not knowing much about the background of his mysterious female flying companion, and asks, somewhat apprehensively, "Where was that?"

Quint stands and walks past Jimmy to sit nearer to him on the seaplane's extended wheel. He lowers his voice a touch and glances toward the path cut through the brush leading to the main house. "I believe she's probably the same Alexa Reid most folks have read about in the newspapers. Not only is she a famed archaeologist, but a notorious treasure huntress, which is a big no, no."

Jimmy gives an odd, sidelong look at Quint and asks, "Which part is the fault... Treasure hunter or archeologist? You've dabbled across the line."

"The occupation is fine; it's the newspapers and local government knowing about what you do that makes it tricky. I don't know how well-informed you are with what she's up to this time around, but you know enough to hide your airplane from sight."

Quint glances up to the lush canopy of palms and jungle trees obscuring the seaplane from view as he ponders. He pulls a long cigar from his shirt pocket and inspects it. "Only repairs I see on this old bird are the fresh bullet holes... not to mention, you looking like you've been worked over real good fairly recent." The barefoot islander strikes a match along the rough pad of his heel and lights the tip of the cigar. He takes several puffs and blows out the smoke in a transcendental halo.

"Now, what kind of trouble have you gotten yourself into this time, Jimmy boy?"

Jimmy sits up and swings his legs over the edge of the swaying hammock. He wipes the sleep from his eyes and looks at his feet like a child caught in a lie. "Hell, Quint, if I knew anything, I'd tell you. Somehow I got mixed up with this lady, and now a one-eyed pirate captain, named Rasmus, has a price on my head."

"Captain P. M. Rasmus? That's a bad crowd to get mixed up with. What does he want?"

Jimmy tilts his head and looks to Quint, as the islander calmly smokes his hand-rolled cigar while leaning back against the wheel-strut of the seaplane. "Damned if I know. Something she knows, I guess?"

A lazy smoke ring escapes from Quint's pursed lips, and he taps it with the glowing end of his cigar.

"Or something she has?"

His feet planted in the sand, Jimmy pulls himself out of the hammock. He strolls over to the sleek body of his beloved seaplane and looks up to the recently inflicted bullet holes.

"Could be…"

Quint adjusts his leg as it hangs over the tire of the amphibious aircraft. "Where are you supposed to take her?"

"An island not far from here."

Crinkling his forehead, Quint smiles with amusement. "That narrows it down to a few dozen. Which one?"

"Some uncharted island coordinates… North by northwest of here."

Jimmy walks over to the driftwood bench seat, stretches his back, and sits. The barefoot islander follows, straining his feet through the beachy sand and stopping to stand before Jimmy. Quint puffs on his cigar and thinks a bit. "The only uncharted island in this area I can think of, that is any size worth visiting, is *Ile Araignee*, or Spider Island for you non-natives."

Jimmy looks up at Quint and cringes at the name. "Should I even ask?"

"The French named it. There's a reason no one goes on that one and it's not on most of the nautical charts. It crawls with noxious spiders. Bunches of 'em."

Jimmy smiles, and they exchange an amused laugh. "Hell, I'll stay in the plane surrounded by ocean, and she can go tromping around for whatever she wants in there."

Quint sits on the driftwood, next to Jimmy, and offers him a cigar from his pocket. The pilot takes it, and Quint affectionately pats Jimmy's shoulder. "That's not too bad of an idea, staying behind. Most of 'em are said to be very aggressive."

Jimmy rolls the long cigar between his fingers, sniffs it, and nibbles the end off. "Maybe she's looking for a pet?"

"Perhaps... She runs with a dangerous crowd."

Quint strikes a match with his thumbnail, lets it flare, and offers Jimmy the lit stick. The rolled tobacco flares, as Jimmy puffs the cigar until it retains its glow, before tranquilly sitting back. Under the palms, the two enjoy the cooling breeze as the color of the evening sky begins to change. Watching the rich tones of the coming sunset, Jimmy looks over at Quint enjoying his smoke. Jimmy watches his trusted adviser and contemplates on his difficult situation. "So, what did you do with her?"

Quint gives one last puff on the lit stick of tobacco and then mashes out the glowing tip on the edge of the driftwood. The remainder of the rolled leaves crumble in his calloused fingers, and he sprinkles the flaky remnants to the breeze.

"She's asleep in my bed."

Jimmy gives Quint a sidelong glance, and the savvy lothario grins at his younger companion. "Relax, my friend. She was exhausted, so I offered it to her. I know better than to get mixed up with that kind of woman, and so should you."

Jimmy takes a long drag on the stogie and exhales while looking off to the low sun in the sky.

"What kind of woman is that?"

"Pure trouble, and you shouldn't even have to ask." Quint bends down and scoops up a double handful of sand. He sifts the soft grains gently across his open palms and sorts out a tiny sea shell from the mixture of broken coral. Rubbing the tiny shell between his fingertips, Quint glances at Jimmy. "You know, a bunch of years ago, sometime during the war, her father disappeared in these very same islands."

"No... I didn't know about that."

Jimmy stands and walks to the empty hammock setup. He sits on the edge of the slung canvas and thinks a moment before pushing back onto it. The bemused pilot lets his feet dangle, as the roped cradle swings.

"Everyone seems to know all about this mysterious woman and her family history except me, and it's really starting to piss me off."

"Like who?"

"Cutter said some things about her."

Quint gestures to the lumped bruise under Jimmy's swollen eye. Jimmy nods as Quint chuckles in amusement and continues. "You are fortunate to run in different circles and know different types of people. During the war, her father had a hell of a time keeping down his reputation as being a treasure-hunting pirate."

"Was he?"

"Pretty much. On the European front, it was paintings; in the islands, it's colonial remnants. We all do things in war that seem right at the time."

Jimmy takes a puff on his cigar and gives himself a push from the sand, swinging the low-slung hammock. "That's great. I'm on the run with the swashbuckler's daughter."

"I don't know what you're thinking of doing with her, but that Rasmus character and his gang are bad ones, I hear. The sooner you can dump this cargo and get clear, the better. Quint lets his gaze travel to the seaplane. "This is probably a flight assignment you don't want to stick through to the end. The islander looks in the direction of his shack and then out to the open water beyond the beach. "You can stay here for a bit, but no offense, I hope you don't stay long."

Jimmy nods his head to his old friend and mentor. "Yeah, I understand."

Puffing on his cigar, Jimmy sighs and lies back deeper in the canvas hammock. Quint watches him awhile, and then looks down at the pink shell between his fingers. A rush of wind comes off the water, and Quint tucks strands of long hair behind his ears. Gazing out to the vacant seascape, he seems disconcerted and tosses the empty shell aside.

Chapter 12

The waves gently lap on the isolated shore, as Quint and Curtiss lie out, relaxed, on the warm, granules of sandy beach. They lounge, gazing skyward, enjoying the late-day cooler temperatures, as the orange orb of the sun nears the horizon. A dark bottle of rum is propped in the sand between them. Arching his spine, Quint peers into the trees toward his pal, Jimmy, still asleep in the hammock hung under the seaplane. With a smile, he shakes his head.

Quint rolls onto his side and props himself up on an elbow. The suntanned islander lifts the bottle, takes a swig, and splashes a little in the palm of his hand. Curtiss continues lying back, but reaches over and dips his furry finger in the rum before licking it.

In the distance, a rumbling sound tickles the air. Quint's ears perk as he dumps the rum out of his hand before standing to peer toward the horizon. Curtiss sits up and shakes the sand from his fur. Listening intently, the engine sound of an airplane can be heard faintly on the breeze.

"I'll be damned… "

Quint sprints barefoot up the beach to the seaplane and flips Jimmy from the hammock. The sleeping pilot hits the sand and comes up spitting mad.

"You asshead, what's yer deal?"

Already at a nearby palm tree, Quint rips fronds from the stalk. In a confused huff, still wiping the sand from his face and chest, Jimmy watches, confused.

"What are you doing?"

With several branches in hand, Quint tosses a large frond over the high winged airplane and points to the sky. "Saving you, stupid. Listen!"

The large radial airplane engines can be faintly heard, clearly getting closer. Jimmy stands, paused in shock, with sand still stuck on his face. "It can't be… How could they?"

"You better believe it, Jimbo. Help me cover over this airplane of yours." Quint tosses another palm leaf over the wing and rushes to tear off more branches.

Jimmy climbs inside the side hatch of the seaplane and comes out with a pair of leather-sheathed machetes. He tosses one to Quint, then jumps down with the other blade and throws the sheath aside. They quickly hack at the lower branches of the nearest palms and other leafy vegetation, using it to cover over and camouflage the beached seaplane.

The distant sound of approaching airplane engines can be clearly heard now. Alexa, in an alerted panic, runs down the jungle path from the house and stops at the clearing. "Jimmy, it's them!"

The seaplane looks to be under a landscaper's trim-pile, and Alexa gawks dumbfounded. She looks up at Jimmy standing on the top of the amphibious aircraft, as he positions the final touches of vegetative disguise. She watches as Quint throws up several more branches. "What are you doing? We have to get out of here."

With his machete in one hand and a palm frond in the other, Jimmy looks down at Alexa. "We're not going anywhere until they pass by here."

"You're kidding me?" As Curtiss peeks out from the hatch of the airplane, Alexa continues while looking out to the ocean waters. "What if they don't pass?"

"They will." Jimmy frowns. "I hope…"

Quint pulls Alexa from the edge of the clearing to concealment under the leaf-draped wing and speaks to her. "There are too many islands around here to stop at every one. They're only trying to spot the airplane."

Alexa peers out from under the hanging fronds and tries to sight the position of the aircraft overhead. Quint leans back against the seaplane wheel-strut and turns his inquiring gaze directly at her. She glances over at him to see his keen eyes bore through her, as he knowingly folds his arms across his chest. His head cants to the side, and he combs loose locks of hair behind an ear with a single finger.

"Tell me again… What kind of research are you doing here in the islands?" His eyes dart skyward, as the thundering sound of the twin-engine airplane steadily approaches above them. She tries to feign innocence at first, then looks away, accepting that her deception has been discovered.

A machete twirls through the air from above and sticks in the palm littered ground. Jimmy ungracefully leaps from the top of the seaplane to the sandy beach and stumbles, as he dashes under the wing to cover. Alexa practically catches him in her arms, and they exchange a look of awkward closeness. He stands, locking eyes with her a moment, as she continues to embrace him. As the sound of the aircraft nears, he pulls her closer.

A black PBY Catalina seaplane buzzes over the island, low enough to rattle and sway the tall palm trees in its wake. Under the cover of the airplane wing, they wait and listen, as the roar of the radial engines fade for a moment before recommencing as they circle back.

Alexa gently, but firmly, tries to ease herself out of Jimmy's arms and whispers, "Did they see us?"

Continuing to hold her tight, turning an ear skyward, Jimmy exchanges a skeptical look with Quint. "They're probably making a second pass to be sure."

A long minute passes, as they each hold their breath in dreaded anticipation of the pirate seaplane coming back again. The pirate Catalina seaplane buzzes the island a second time, and they watch as it banks slightly in the sky directly over Quint's elaborately constructed beach shack. The sound of the aircraft continues to fade in the distance, and all three quietly breathe a sigh of relief.

Quint rests his head of long hair back against the seaplane's metal frame and chuckles. "Jimmy, you've always been a lucky bastard."

Jimmy's eyes meet Alexa's a moment, and he smiles. Suddenly feeling extremely awkward in Jimmy's arms, Alexa pulls herself away and steps from under the covered wing.

"Is it safer to head out tonight or tomorrow?"

Jimmy rolls his eyes at her single-minded persistence. He turns to Quint and notices a look of concern, as the long-haired sailor studies the curved underbelly of the flying-boat. "What is it, Quint?"

The seasoned islander runs his hand along the deep, stepped hull of the flying boat and stops to look up at Jimmy with a troubled expression. "If that island you're going to is in fact Spider Island, you're going to have a hell of a time hiding this plane. It's not a friendly island to access... No beaches."

Alexa walks back toward Quint under the high wing and stands before him. "What do you mean, Spider Island?" She turns and shoots a cold, betrayed stare over at Jimmy. "Captain Ferral, you promised to tell no one."

Flustered and angry, Jimmy turns around to face Alexa. "Hold on there, missy. I didn't tell him a thing. How could I say anything when you haven't told *me* diddly squat?"

"And it's a good thing I didn't, bucket-mouth!"

Quint stands from his crouched position and takes a step away from the seaplane. He rubs his whiskered chin, as Jimmy and Alexa gaze crossly at the other. With a cough and an exaggerated clearing of his throat, he gains their attention. "Jimmy's right. He hasn't told me much of anything. But, in point, if that is the uncharted island where you're headed, you're gonna have problems. That landmass is more or less a big pile of rocks surrounded by marshy seaweed that keeps everyone away from it. Your plane would get bogged down or torn up by the jagged pillars just under the surface, close at shore."

Quint watches the two silently listening and then continues. "Before you two explorers go to killing each other on my beach, in the house I have some island-charts of the area that we can use to pinpoint your destination, to be sure." The argumentative pair stand before the islander, exchange a consensual look, and then nod their agreement. When they move to follow Quint down the path to the house, he puts up his hands to stop them. "Whatever the destination, I want your guarantee that you will be off this island and out of my hair by morning. I have no desire to invite a squadron of gun-toting air pirates to my peaceful abode."

Alexa nods and turns to Jimmy, who sets his jaw, resolved. "I'll have her off your island by morning."

Quint smiles and gestures to the house. "Okay then, let's have a look at some charts and coordinates."

Alexa steals a look toward Jimmy, who shakes his head and follows her on the path to Quint's rustic island mansion.

Chapter 13

The inside of Quint's remote island villa is a mix of wartime military surplus and custom island carpentry. There are metal, wood, and canvas supply items bearing the stamps of the U.S. and other far-flung countries, joined with carved native driftwood to make cabinets, tables, and chairs. The primitive surroundings are highlighted by dozens of homemade candles and strategically placed polished reflectors to boost the luminosity of the flaming light.

Quint pulls some rolled charts from a series of stacked tubes and opens them on a wide, palm-log table. He looks up at Alexa in the candlelight, and his eyes flicker with intrigue. "How about those specific coordinates, Alexa?"

Alexa pulls a folded slip of paper from her breast pocket and slides the course-plotting figures across the table to the edge of the navigational chart. With an excited twinkle in his eye, Quint looks at Jimmy and then turns back to Alexa. He opens the paper and stares at it a moment before plotting points on the map before him.

Jimmy watches over Quint's shoulder, then walks to the corner where Curtiss relaxes in a lounge chair. He glances back toward the two figures hovering over the table and grunts. "What's the verdict, Quint?"

Quint pauses and then peers across the table at Alexa. He turns to Jimmy and shakes his head solemnly. "Sorry pal, *Ile Araignee,* on the money."

Jimmy mumbles a curse under his breath, and Alexa leans down for a closer inspection of the hand-sketched portion of the map. "Are the alterations to this map accurate?"

"They are. Made 'em myself."

Alexa sighs and comments, "With that shoreline, how close can we get and still be able to pull out again?"

Quint looks up at her earnestly and moves his index finger on the chart around the enhanced detail of the island. "Maybe a hundred yards or so in that deep-hulled seaplane. It's gonna be a tough swim through the marshy tide-water and, if you make it to that island, your ride is going to be a sitting duck out in the open until you fly out of there again."

Staring at the details of the map, Alexa's mind churns for options. "Where are we now?"

Resting his other hand on the map, Quint extends a lean, knuckled finger and taps the exact location of his island. He glances up at her and seems to follow her train of thought.

Alexa traces the path between the two isles and, in a hushed tone, speaks to Quint. "What about a boat?"

The islander cracks a smile. He looks over at Jimmy sitting near Curtiss, grumbling to himself quietly while only half-listening. "You could maneuver right up to the island with the right type of boat. Trouble is, you don't have one."

Finally, the mention of a boat catches Jimmy's attention. He walks over to the map table and looks down at the distance between the two landmasses. Alexa stares at him a telling moment, then turns to Quint.

"You do."

Both hands on the table, Quint's hair falls forward as he nods his head slowly. "Yup, and I'd like to keep it afloat. Getting mixed up with Rasmus and his pirates isn't on my list of ways to enjoy a long life."

Alexa puts on her most persuasive charm and bends low on the table, leaning forward toward Quint. She looks at the islander with eyes that glimmer with excitement. Her womanly features glow sultry in the candlelight and a tinge of electricity fills the air. "It should be a simple slip in and out. You'll be paid well and compensated if anything more than a scratch should happen to your boat. Please, Quint... We need you."

The experienced sailor takes in her convincing display with his penetrating eyes. He pushes back from the table and flashes his own charming grin through whiskered features. Quint shakes back the long silver strands of hair from his face and hooks a thumb toward Jimmy. "That sweet-talk package may work on my friend Jim there, but I'll need a little more to go on before I stick my neck out for you. Good luck to you, honey." He turns and shakes his head, amused, but guarded.

"Jimmy, she's dangerous. The sooner you get her out of here, the better for all of us."

Alexa watches as Quint moves to his makeshift bar and pours himself a drink. She angles for support from Jimmy, who shrugs his shoulders. Filled with an unquenchable determination, Alexa stares down at the map. She calculates the remaining distance to her ultimate objective and clenches her jaw before speaking, "What do you need to know?"

The clank of a stirring spoon on the edge of a glass tumbler breaks the silence, and Quint glances across the room. He swirls his drink in hand and takes a long sip before walking back over to Alexa at the table. The rolled chart and the scrap of paper with the island coordinates captivate him, and he ponders the dangerous consequences involved. Quint's gaze travels across the room to Curtiss lounging in the corner, then over to Jimmy innocently standing nearby, and finally turn directly on Alexa.

"You'll have to tell me everything."

"Everything?"

"You can swim it, as far as I'm concerned."

The island host raises an eyebrow inquisitorially, and Alexa slowly nods in surrendered agreement.

~*~

The hazy moisture of dawn hangs in the air as the sun crests behind the watered horizon. The elevated wooden path creaks, from the weight of feet shuffling, with the weight of supplies. Toward the end of the narrow pier, Quint stands on his tethered sailboat, bringing gear aboard for the island-hopping excursion.

In the dim light of morning, Jimmy hands the veteran mariner items from the accumulated supplies on the dock. They both look to the distant path coming from the house and watch, as Alexa walks down the beach with her arms loaded. Quint continues to stash the gear aboard, and Jimmy holds out another leather-strapped duffle bag, waiting for him to take it. "Why are you doing this, Quint?"

Quint stands and faces him, putting his bare foot to the rail of the boat. "Because, I want to."

They glance down the dock at Alexa and Jimmy sighs, "She makes a good argument, putting our asses on the line, but I could just fly her outta here and take whatever comes. We could be gone and keep you clear of the whole thing."

Quint chortles a low laugh and continues his gaze down the dock, as Alexa saunters toward them. "You're my friend. I was curious. I figured you'd still follow it through and do the damned thing whether I helped or not."

Jimmy nods and hands another canvas duffle bag over to Quint. "Yeah, I guess you're right."

The sailor tosses the bag in the hatch of the compartment below and turns to face Jimmy. "I'd rather have the fun of being along for the jaunt than pick up the broken pieces later. I don't have many friends." He glances up at Alexa approaching on the dock. "And, it's clear you care about her."

Jimmy looks past his shoulder at her and back to Quint. "No, it's not like that."

Alexa drops the bags she was carrying near the other pile of supplies, and wipes the sweat from her forehead as she stands next to Jimmy. "What are you two talking about?"

Quint chuckles and swings on the sail rigging down onto the deck of the boat. "Not much... Just you."

Alexa tugs at her sweat-dampened, form-hugging shirt. "Oh yeah, and how's that?"

Quint calls out, "How you're growing on him."

The sun peeks above the horizon, sending rays of light across the ocean waters, and Jimmy wobbles his head with feigned embarrassment. He looks at Alexa's glowing and radiant beauty in the early morning light and tries to conceal his confused emotions. "He's joking. It's not like that."

Her eyes seem to smile at him with a mysterious, but sensual, warmth. "How is it then?"

"I just want to help... see this thing through."

Alexa winks, and, in a slightly teasing tone, exclaims, "And be paid."

Uncomfortable with his conflicted feelings for her, Jimmy nods as he notices Curtiss poke his head from the forward hatch of the sailboat. The smell of the sea and the sway of the dock put Jimmy in a strange sense of unbalance. The pilot glances toward his concealed seaplane on the beach, then grabs another bag of gear and tosses it aboard.

"Yeah, and get paid."

Jimmy helps Alexa across the railing of the boat and hands the remaining supplies from the dock over to Quint. After dropping several stuffed sacks into the cabin below, Quint casts his narrowed eyes toward the morning sun blazing on the horizon. "Aye, Captain Jim. We set sail for uncharted waters on the quick."

Walking to the ship's bow, Jimmy unties the sailing vessel from its tethered mooring, pushes off, and hops aboard. "All clear."

Quint positions himself behind the ship's wheel rudder and looks skyward to the bare, sail rigging. "All right, Maties, let's hoist some cloth and be on our way."

The small crew works together at hoisting sails. Jimmy is impressed as Alexa ties off ship knots like a seasoned naval cadet. He glances back at Quint who notices as well, and they exchange an admiring glance. Alexa perceives Jimmy watching her in the rigging and flashes him a confident smile. He feels a slight flush in his features, as he makes his way toward her along the ship's deck. "You've done this sort of thing before?"

Alexa finishes tying off the tether line and gazes up. "Not since I was a little kid, but I have a pretty good memory for such things."

"You're an old hand at it."

"I come from a line of seafaring adventurers."

Alexa looks away from Jimmy's enamored gaze and addresses Quint at the helm. "How long do you think it will be until we get there?"

Quint sits back with his foot hoisted on the ship-wheel and looks to the clouds in the sky. "Depending on the winds, we should pull in tomorrow, late morning."

~*~

The single-mast, wooden sailing sloop has full canvas pulling it across glimmering ocean waters. Quint maintains their course with a compass and chart tucked under his leg. Emerging from the compartment below, Jimmy looks to Quint who nods ahead toward the deck.

Alexa sits at the front of the boat, letting the steady breath of the wind envelope her as she gazes out at the watery horizon. Curtiss curls up cozily next to her, and the fur along his body swirls with the breeze. The boat cants into the wind, as Jimmy eases his way around the cabin and then slides in next to Curtiss and Alexa. "Can I join you?"

Alexa turns with a beaming radiance from the sea air. She smiles and scoots over to make more space for him to sit. "Sure thing, Captain Ferral."

Jimmy looks out, watching the bow of the boat rise and fall against the skyline, and crosses his arms in contemplation. The wind blows steady and Alexa glances over at him, seeing his thoughts at work. "What's on your mind, Captain?"

Turning to her, he smiles and leans back on his elbows. "What does this Polynesian King's treasure look like, exactly? I mean, how big is it?"

Alexa reaches down to the pack at her feet and pulls out a leather-bound journal. She thumbs through it, looking at her research. "I don't know for sure."

Jimmy peers over at the book and sees pages full of scribbles and detailed sketches. "What if it's too large to move off the island?"

She traces a finger along one of the pages, scanning through drawings and notations. Alexa mumbles to herself as she tries to find what she's looking for in the descriptions. Curtiss, no longer receiving her attentions, sits up and notices Alexa's open bag. He hops to the deck, next to the newfound attraction, steals a glance at her, and peeks inside.

Jimmy stares out again to the horizon and breathes in the warm, salty air. "If it is that valuable, I'd think you'd have done a bit more research or remembered how big it was."

She looks at him enticingly. "It's not about size."

At their feet, Curtiss pokes his arm into Alexa's bag, snatches out some skimpy undergarments, and pulls them over his head like an eye-patch. Alexa quickly grabs the skimpy panties from Curtiss, pushes them back into her bag, and closes it. Despite embarrassment and Jimmy's laughter, Alexa throws a scolding glance at Curtiss who hangs his head in shame. She looks over at Jimmy and their eyes connect briefly with an unspoken yearning. Jimmy contemplates his feelings for her and then smiles, jokingly. "I thought he looked just like ol' Captain Rasmus."

"I don't even want to think about him."

She stifles a shiver and looks back down at her journal. "Anyway, back to your question. I know that before the treasure was removed from *Iles Tuamotu*, the Polynesian King carried it with him always."

Jimmy gives Curtiss a shooing pat to his tail and the monkey scoots over the roof of the cabin and swings below. He watches Quint navigating at the helm and turns to Alexa.

"Whatever size it is, it's probably worth a lot of coconuts, considering the interested parties."

Alexa leans her head back and rests it on the cabin wall. She closes her eyes and lets the gentle sway of the sailing ship relax her mind. Watching her features glow in the sunlight, Jimmy enjoys the quiet, peaceful sight of her female figure. Her head rocks slightly, and she lets out a deep sigh.

"Jimmy, I'm glad you're in this with me. You've been a pretty good sport through it all."

Alexa opens her bright green eyes and turns her head toward him. He looks away, self-conscious of his feelings toward her, and nods. "Sure, no big deal."

She notices as he sits awkwardly, in her gaze. "This started out as just another treasure hunt and turned into quite the mess."

A splashing spray of water comes over the bow and Jimmy smiles at her reassuringly. "Welcome to the South Pacific."

Chapter 14

An early morning fog drifts past the sailing sloop as the daybreak sun burns the crisp, ocean air to a salt-tinged mist. Curtiss stands beside Quint at the helm, and the boat rocks jauntily through the rolling waters. The two angular sails blow taut in the steady breeze, and laps of water peel back from the painted wood hull.

The cabin hatch opens, and Jimmy pops his head out from below. He lets his eyes adjust to the early light of day, and Curtiss slides across the deck into Jimmy's open arms. Quint smiles, standing in a sailor pose behind the ship-wheel. "Good morning, Jimmy-boy."

"Mornin', Quint. Do you want me to take the wheel a while, so you can get some rest?"

Quint looks down at his ocean navigational chart and compass bearing, making slight adjustments to the rudder accordingly. "No thanks, we should be there in an hour or so. It's a pretty small speck of land on a large canvas of water." The sailor peers at the sun, then back to the compass heading. He shoots a sidelong glance to

Jimmy as the seaplane pilot, looking much more rested, climbs on deck. "Can't have you at the helm and miss the damn thing. Be another day or two circling and trying to find it again."

Curtiss jumps aside to the rigging while Jimmy clings to a line, leaning out over the port-side rail. The steady breeze washes over him, and he stretches his shoulders back to stare at the vast ocean and then to his seafaring pal. "Your confidence in me is touching."

"There's a reason you fly, remember?"

Jimmy slides into a seat near the helm and catches the warming sun. With a cynical squint of an eye, Jimmy gives a fleeting look toward Quint. "I got us lost… Once."

"Six days I'll never forget."

Closing his eyes, Jimmy scratches his messy hair and relaxes into the steady rise and fall of the boat on the swells. With the exception of the rush of the water and occasional slap of the wooden hull on the surface, the creak of the rigging is all that is heard.

The familiar rumbling of airplane engines in the distance breaks the friends from their peaceful musings. In shocked disbelief, they hold their breath and strain to listen, their ears pinned to the breeze. The faint sound becomes more distinctive and Jimmy bolts upright, turning to face Quint. "You think that's them again…?"

"You bet it is. They're not gonna stop or give up."

"How would they know we're here?"

Shading his narrowed eyes from the sun, Quint quickly scans the vessel to identify any signs of passengers or cargo. "They don't yet… But they sure will if you don't get yourself and that hirsute copilot below. Grab that loose duffle and toss it down too!"

With a calling whistle, Jimmy waves Curtiss from the rigging and hurries toward the cabin hatch. He grabs the loaded gear bag on the way and ushers his copilot below deck. Jimmy drops the bag down the short-laddered set of steps and slides the storm hatch closed, as he moves to the space below. At the ship's wheel, Quint reaches over and trims the sails, as the sound of the approaching aircraft engines echo off the blue seas.

In the ship's cabin, Jimmy slips down the ladder and lets his eyes adjust to the dim light. Alexa appears before him, recently awakened and attentive to his hurried action.

"What is it Jimmy, is something happening?"

Jimmy steps away from the ladder and politely looks away as she drapes a linen shirt over her tank top.

"It's them. They'll be overhead in a minute."

"Both of them?"

Jimmy tosses the gear bag on the small table, unzips it, and pulls out his .45 auto handgun. He checks the 1911's clip, racks the slide to chamber a round, and puts on the safety.

"I don't know. We heard engines in the distance. There's still a bit of a morning fog."

"Then maybe they won't see us."

Jimmy looks over at her skeptically.

"They've probably already spotted us."

"What are you going to do?"

Easing up a few steps on the ladder, Jimmy peers out from the concealment of the hatch and tries to listen for any sounds in the morning sky. "They haven't touched down. They'll probably just pass overhead, mapping a search grid pattern of the area."

Alexa steps on the ladder behind him, about to speak, and Jimmy puts his hand out to silence her. "Shh, be quiet." He strains to make out the sounds of the radial engines or the telling splash of an open-water landing from the approaching pirate seaplane. He glances back at her, and they exchange a trepidatious look of uneasiness.

~*~

At the helm, watching, Quint studies the black-painted PBY Catalina seaplane dropping in altitude over the horizon. He murmurs aloud, "Haven't seen one of those in a while." The mariner glances over and slides his bare foot atop a coil of ropes on the deck, concealing the pistol nestled in the center.

The heavily-armed navy seaplane buzzes over the boat, nearly taking the wind from the sails. The rumble of the engines and the whirl of spinning propellers cause the sailing sloop to shudder to the keel and ripple the ocean waters. Quint stands and watches as the flying warship roars past and rises into the sky, continuing off into the distance.

~*~

Inside the pirate PBY Catalina, a radio operator sits behind the pilot's chair adjusting his headphones before tapping the button on the microphone receiver. The roar of the dual engines reverberates off the metal hull, as the seaplane gains altitude after flying low along the ocean's surface. "Catalina P. M. R., this is A. P. Two-Twenty. Do you copy?"

A wide-shouldered, stone-faced man in a trim-fitting suit coat suddenly fills the oval cockpit doorway. His piercing eyes are as dark as his short-cropped hair. The radio operator glances up at the looming presence and quickly offers him a listen on the spare headset.

There is radio silence and then a slight crackle of static. The two pilots behind the flight controls listen intently while watching out the windows. They fly in a wide arcing circle, keeping sight of the small sailing sloop in the waters below.

"This is Catalina P. M. R., Go ahead."

The radioman gazes up at the man in the doorway who nods as he holds the headphones up to his ear. "The sailing sloop you identified prior is en route to unknown destination. The vessel was observed from air to have single occupant and no visible cargo. Over."

The radio crackles quietly over the continuous roar of the engines, as the seaplane travels onward. Finally, the static dissipates, and Rasmus' flagship returns to the radio. "Chart course of identified sloop and continue search within striking distance. Will make contact and examine island of origin further. Over."

The radio operator looks up into the dark, piercing eyes of the suited man standing over him. He receives a nod and breathes a reply into the microphone. "Copy that, this is A. P. Two-Twenty, signing out."

The man in the suit drops the headset to the navigator's table and stares through the windshield into the pale blue morning sky. The radial engines rumble as he abruptly turns from the doorway and disappears into the hold of the air-pirate vessel.

Chapter 15

The early haze of morning has burned off, and the sun sits high in the clear skies. Slicing through dark blue waters that turn spotted with patches of luminescent aqua-blue, the sloop sails on. Sitting with Curtiss in the shade of the sailcloth, Alexa glances over at Jimmy and Quint near the helm. Catching her eye with a passing look, Quint leans over the chart and makes a mark. She watches, as he adjusts their direction and steers the boat using the wind.

With a set of binoculars raised to his face, Jimmy starts to crack a smile as the faint outline of a landmass comes into view on the horizon. "Alexa, there's your uncharted island."

Holding Curtiss's small hand, she walks across the ship deck and exchanges the hairy copilot for an opportunity to look through the distance glasses. "How long before we reach the shoreline?"

"What do you think, Quint?"

Quint looks up to the taut sails and deftly commands the ship-wheel in concert with the rise and fall of the ocean swells. "If this wind doesn't change, it shouldn't be long."

With a relieved smile, Alexa hands the field glasses back to Jimmy and moves toward the passenger cabin below. At the open hatch, she takes a few steps down the ladder and turns to him with her face full of excitement. "C'mon Jimmy, let's get our gear together."

Jimmy turns to Quint, then, confused, looks to Alexa. "What do you mean *our* gear? I'm not setting foot on that deathtrap of an island."

Taken aback, Alexa's enthusiasm turns to disdain. "Why is that, Captain Ferral?"

Jimmy looks to Quint for any words of support, but all he gets is a knowing grin. Frustrated, he grabs a ship line, pulls himself to his feet, and walks the top deck toward Alexa. He stands over her at the hatch, as she holds the handrail midway down. "*Spider Island* isn't just a cute name for it. You're not paying me to go traipsing through the jungle on a treasure hunt to get killed by a mob of poisonous arachnids."

"What exactly am I paying you for?"

He jabs an irate finger toward the island on the horizon, as his temper flares. "To get you *to* that island."

Unflinching, Alexa looks up at the hired seaplane pilot, then to the ship-deck and then to the sails, snapping in the breeze. "I may be mistaken… But as I recall, that is why I had to hire your pal, Quint."

Jimmy reddens with indignation as Alexa smirks, turns away from him, and descends into the boat cabin.

He grips both hands to the side of the cabin hatch and yells down at her. "I'm your ride back to civilization once you find what you came here for! I'm your damn ticket out of here... which I hope happens soon!"

At the bottom step, Alexa calmly turns back to Jimmy. "You would think you'd want to keep me alive on that island, so you can get your damned money." She steps off the ladder and mumbles loudly enough for him to hear. "Of course, you're too dimwitted to even think that far ahead."

Jimmy fumes silently, as he holds on the wooden hatch rails and stares down at the dark cabin. He looks back at Quint, who flashes another one of his perceptive smiles, as Curtiss skirts along the deck and swings through one of the open portal windows. Feeling betrayed by his furry copilot companion, Jimmy looks again to his sailor friend, who flops his wrist over the ship-wheel and shrugs.

"She's paid me already, brother."

Clenching his fists, Jimmy lets out a growl of curses, as he marches toward the port bow and circles the cabin.

~*~

Jimmy descends the ladder into the lower cabin and begins to rummage through his gear bag. Alexa stares at him and attempts to hide her pleasure. "What are you doing?"

"I'm going with you."

"Don't bother. I don't need your help."

He digs through his backpack and lays out items on the narrow bunk. "I know. I'm going anyway."

The cabin rocks gently with the ocean swells and she smiles teasingly. "What about all the scary spiders?"

Jimmy looks up at her and tucks his pistol in his waistband. "I love spiders... Can't get enough of 'em."

In a final show of annoyance, Jimmy shivers and then breaks to a fleeting sneer. Alexa slings her leather-strapped canvas bag over her shoulder and moves a step closer to him. "Thank you, Jimmy. It means a lot to me."

"Yeah, don't mention it."

His heartbeat quickens, as she brushes past him and climbs up the ladder to the deck. Her pleasing scent lingers and he watches her slender silhouetted exit the upper hatch. Jimmy puts a hand across his chin and tries to clear his mind from the fleeting thought of following her into much worse predicaments.

~*~

Guided by Quint's skillful handling and watchful eye, the small sailing craft eases through marsh-covered waters. The subaquatic coastline of sharp lava-rock is revealed in the slow wake of the wooden sloop. They watch over the side, noticing, in the clear areas, knife-like stone pillars looming close to the water's surface. The boat nears the overgrown and rock-strewn coastline, as Jimmy and Alexa wait anxiously at the starboard bow.

Jimmy hears a scraping sound against the wooden hull, while the boat slides gently through the shrouded waters. "Hey Quint, will you be able to get us right up to it?"

With fierce concentration, Quint adjusts the remaining sail cloth and senses the route of the wooden vessel through the soles of his bare feet. "I'll get you as near as possible...." He breaks his concentration with a fleeting thought and grins. "You'll be swimming distance, at least."

Alexa follows Jimmy's look over the side at the thick growth of slimy seaweed covering the gently heaving waters. They exchange a look of dread at the thought of trying to swim through it. He looks back at Quint and gestures a supporting wave. "Do the best you can... Closer, the better."

A rope whistles through the block and tackle, and the mainsail collapses as Quint guides the slow-moving craft. Suddenly, the hull drags heavily as it rubs along the rocky coast, and the boat seems to stick tight, coming to a firm stop. Quint steps away from the now, useless ship-wheel, and walks to the forward bow, where Jimmy and Alexa stand waiting. "Well, here we are."

Alexa fastens another button on her linen blouse and looks at the unwelcoming coastal terrain a few feet away. "Are we stuck?"

Quint gazes over the side of the boat into the treacherous waters below. "For now, yes." He turns to them, "This is as close as I can get you with the coming of low tide. It may drop a bit more yet, but it should be on the way back up in a few hours."

Jimmy looks past the wet, rocky shoreline and notices that the island terrain is thick with vines and low, clinging undergrowth. "It's a good thing we brought the machetes."

The long-haired sailor rests his hands on his hips and grunts in reply, "Where's a blow torch when you need it?"

Jimmy holds one of the lines from the sail rigging and ushers his other hand toward Alexa and the short hop to land. "Shall we say, ladies first?"

The treasure hunter looks at her hired companion and smiles warmly. "After you, Captain."

"Yeah, that's what I figured."

Jimmy swings his arms out ahead of his body and takes a flying leap, hurtling himself outward to the rocky shoreline. He lands firmly on a stone ledge and then stumbles a few steps farther inland. Instantly, his boots sink ankle deep in the soft mud, and he falls sideways into the slimy muck.

"Aww, hell..."

The suctioning sound of feet in moist sludge follows, as Jimmy grabs onto some vinery and pulls himself to more stable ground. Quint stands at the starboard bow, laughing, while lifting Curtiss up and holding him on his hip. "That's it, Jimbo, pull yerself out of that mess. The whole island is probably made up of that stuff, so watch it."

Jimmy looks at Alexa as she gets ready to make the leap. "Toss me your bag first."

Alexa looks concerned, as she studies the distance over the marshy water. "It has my treasure journal and my notes. Are you going to catch it?"

Jimmy nods and she tosses the backpack across to him. With a quick stretch, he grabs it mid-air, before it slaps into the churned muck. He steps back, as Alexa quickly follows.

She lands both her feet just past the rock ledge, sinking shin-deep in the muck, before falling over to catch herself. Jimmy reaches out to support her body as she lunges forward. Legs encased in the soft mud, she peers up at him gratefully, as she pulls her feet from the sludge and climbs to firmer turf. "Thank you, Jimmy."

"Well, that's what you pay me for."

She feigns a smile at him, puts on her backpack and unsheathes a machete. He holds back, and Alexa doggedly begins slashing through the undergrowth as she makes her way through the jungle. For a short time, Jimmy watches her and then turns back to the boat, where Quint waits on deck.

"You gonna to be here when we get back?"

Jumping from Quint's side, Curtiss climbs high in the ship rigging and strains to see Alexa departing through the foliage. They both look to the climbing monkey, and Quint smiles at Jimmy with a passive shrug. "Jimmy, you worry too much about your friends. Yer ol' pal Curtiss here wouldn't let me leave her stranded. You, maybe... But not her."

"Thanks a lot, Quint."

The weathered sailor leans on the ship rail and brushes back the long strands of his hair. "We'll be stuck right here until the tide comes back in. Things may look different when the water rises, but we'll be around."

"Your reassurance is a comfort."

Jimmy draws his machete from its sheath and turns to follow Alexa into the jungle. Quint gives a sendoff wave and calls out, as Jimmy chops his way through the thick greenery. "Don't pet the spiders, especially the pretty colorful ones!"

He continues to laugh, as Curtiss drops from the sail rigging and into his arms, before clamoring down to the deck. "That's right Curtiss... Jimbo will need to keep sharp eyes." They watch and listen from the bow of the sailboat, as the crashing in the jungle fades and the two fortune hunters disappear into the remote, tropical island forest.

Chapter 16

The island foliage is lush green from trunk to treetop. Arms swinging, they slash a narrow path with their brush knives, as Alexa boldly leads the way. Leafy vines and branches crash aside as the pair heave forward at a steady pace toward a mysterious destination.

Jimmy takes a moment to catch his breath, pausing in Alexa's boot tracks. Streams of sweat run down his face and chest, as he waits cautiously for a colorful, eight-legged beast to completely cross his path. The furry, flower-like arachnid, about the size of a fist, looks up at him inquisitively before it sidesteps away, disappearing into the greenery.

The seaplane pilot gazes back to their ragged-cut trail through the thick jungle and sighs. He wipes the sweat-curled hair back from his brow and murmurs aloud, "What the hell am I doing here?" He feels both mystified and despondent, until he hears Alexa shouting to him from up ahead.

"Captain Ferral, are you still coming?"

"Yeah, but uh ..."

"What's the problem, Captain?"

He shakes off the unsettling image of the large spider and jogs ahead to catch her. "Where exactly are we going?"

Alexa swings her machete and, with a solid thwack, sticks the steel blade into a tree trunk. With her bandana, she wipes the sweat from her face while sliding the backpack off her shoulders. Taking a moment to open her bag, she pulls out the leather-bound notebook.

Jimmy glances down at the treasure journal, but he's quickly distracted by the dozens of spiders that surround them, sunning themselves on trees and rocks. To the casual eye, they appear to be large flowers, until they suddenly bolt into frantic motion. He turns to Alexa as she flips the pages of her notebook and reads.

"My notes say there should be a pile of rocks, like a mountain, with an opening, halfway up near the top."

Cautiously, Jimmy nudges the spider nearest his foot with the blade of his machete and looks around at the piles of random-sized boulders surrounding them.

"The whole island is a pile of rocks."

She flips pages and reads several more notations while ignoring Jimmy's comment. "We are so close to finding it that I can hardly believe it."

"The only thing we seem close to is dying."

The humid island air hangs heavy, as Alexa grimaces, disappointedly, at Jimmy. She tucks the treasure journal away, turns to look around at their rocky surroundings and slides her arms back into the leather straps of the pack.

"We'll know it when we see it."

With renewed determination, Alexa rips the machete from the tree trunk and again starts hacking her way through the congested jungle. She chops a hanging vine from her path and calls back over her shoulder.

"Are you coming, Captain?"

Jimmy shakes his head reluctantly and rests the green-stained blade of his machete on his sweat-soaked shoulder. "Yeah, I'm coming." Following behind her, Jimmy proceeds in the wake of the fanatical archaeologist's trail of leafy debris

~*~

Along the rocky coastline of the spider-infested island, Quint's boat bobs gently in the water. It sits inches above the ominous underwater obstructions that previously impeded the boat's progress. Stretched out on the deck, hands folded behind his head, Quint lounges in the broken shade of the nearby overhanging trees. An insect buzzes past and his eyelids flutter, but his breathing remains heavy and calm.

A warm breeze drifts over him, and his fleeting imaginings of tickling fingers over native island women takes a turn of realism when he is violently jostled from his slumber. Quint jerks awake and sits up to see Curtiss jumping around, screeching a call of warning.

"What... What is it, pal?"

The monkey frantically careens in a circle around the sail rigging, then leaps from the boat-side to the jungle island. Without looking back, the furry copilot scrambles into the thick underbrush and disappears.

Quint blinks the sleep from his eyes and calls out. "Curtiss, what the hell is wrong with you?"

Trying to shake off his lingering drowsiness, Quint moves astern to take a look around. He thinks he can hear the muffled sound of airplane engines, but not from overhead. Tilting his ear to the wind, he listens.

The low rumbling of radials and spinning propellers vibrates across the water and up through the wooden craft. Quint senses the impending danger, as the reverberation transmits through his bare feet.

"Oh, shit!"

Quint rushes to the bow, leaps to the rocky shore, and begins to untie the tether line from a curving palm tree. He hears a rustling in the underbrush behind him and turns. Coiling the rope in hand, he whispers out into the jumble of green vegetation. "Curtiss, is that you?"

The echoing sound of the approaching pirate seaplane distracts him momentarily from his task. Then, moving quickly, Quint tosses the coiled line onboard, freeing the boat. The sound of low, rumbling engines gets louder and more threatening, as the water-bound seaplane travels steadily around the island coast.

Quint turns for a last look into the jungle for Curtiss. Unexpectedly, the left side of his head is met with a solid *crack* from the butt-stock of an automatic rifle. He stumbles back in blinding pain before being knocked out cold by a second jarring blow to his temple. His body spins toward the boat, as he slumps to a rocky patch of hardscape.

Chapter 17

The pinging sound of steel machete blades hacking through tropical vines and leafy branches continues, as the brush-choppers emerge from the jungle into a clearing. They look around at the lava-formed-boulders covered in vegetation. Still holding onto the machete, Alexa lowers her tired arm. With her bandana, she dabs the trickles of sweat streaming down her face and off the tip of her nose.

Stepping around from behind her, Jimmy looks out to the huge mountain of volcanic stones. He gazes up at the steep hillside and groans. "I guess this is your pile of rocks." She points her blade to the top where a crevice forms a dark, crescent-shaped opening. "And there is our entrance."

Green slime runs off the edge of the blade, as Alexa wipes her machete on a leaf. She sheaths the knife and pulls out her treasure journal. The book trembles in her hands, as she thumbs through the pages until she finds her place marker and mumbles aloud. "This is it."

She lowers the book reverently and, with a glowing expression, turns to Jimmy.

"What do you think now, Captain Ferral?"

Jimmy stares at her, wanting to enjoy her beauty and cheery excitement, but reluctantly draws his attention away. He looks to their intended destination on the mountain and concentrates his gaze upon the patchwork of colorful spiders basking in the sun along their path. "I think Captain Rasmus just became the least of our problems. Those colorful things you see out there aren't harmless flowers."

Alexa looks out to the hundreds of spiders dotting the landscape and smiles, undaunted. "No time to stop and smell the roses anyway. We'll just have to keep clear of them."

She closes the treasure journal, tucks it back in her bag, and begins the climbing hike toward the mountain's orifice. Jimmy watches, amazed, as she steps over several basking spiders without concern, focused intently on her sole purpose. Another large, eight-legged creature scurries across Jimmy's path, and he waits for it to pass before moving on.

~*~

The pirate seaplane floats anchored along the coastline, a short distance from Quint's sailboat. In the water beside the open hatch, tied at the port-side of the seaplane, sits a rubber, inflatable dinghy. Two gun-toting air pirates wait obediently in the raft, paddles ready.

A shadowed form appears at the pirate seaplane doorway, and the sharp-featured crew member in the fitted suit looks out toward the stationary sailing ship.

His piercing eyes take in all the details, from hull to masthead, yet his face remains stoic. One of the pirates in the dinghy half-stands and ushers the man to the center bench seat. "Chief Mate Merrill, sir."

Merrill nods affirmative and steps into the waiting raft. He is followed by another air pirate wearing a military flight suit and carrying a .45 automatic Thompson machine gun. Dipping the shortened paddle blades into the marshy water, they splash the dinghy toward the anchored sloop.

As the small rubber raft approaches the sailboat; Quint can be seen on the foredeck, unconscious and slumped over. Blood runs from Quint's forehead wound, as he sits tied to a canvas-slung deck chair. From the inflatable dinghy, Merrill watches with unflinching eyes. He waits until they brush up against the side of the wooden hull before standing and grabbing hold of the knotted rope that dangles over the rail.

His suit coat stretched across broad shoulders, Merrill quickly ascends the side of the sailboat and swings his leg over the deck railing. The chief mate steps aboard gracefully and adjusts the concealed gun rig under his arm. He calmly paces the distance to the captive, who sits, collapsed, in the deck chair.

Like a shark readying to attack, Merrill slowly circles his target. The measured footsteps pause before the slumped prey, and Merrill's palm lashes out, giving Quint a hard slap. With another smack, he backhands the unconscious mariner, to no effect. He barks a command at the nearby crewman. "Wake him up."

A dropped auto-rifle clatters to the rooftop of the ship cabin and the pirate lowers an empty wooden bucket over the side of the boat. As the bucket sinks, the man leans out and watches as the once thick, marshy covering over the water starts to thin and separate as the tide rises. He waits for the bucket to fill and pulls it up. With the sloshing pail in hand, the pirate strides over to the unresponsive figure in the chair and then slings the salty water into Quint's downturned face.

Sputtering and choking back to life, his head pushed aside by the wave of thick seawater, Quint shakes his wet hair and slowly peers up. Merrill takes a commanding stance before him and waits patiently for Quint to regain faculties. The air pirate officer speaks slowly, and matter of fact, despite the harsh introduction. "You have information for us?"

Through his wet mop of hair, Quint glowers at the uninvited pirate crew aboard his boat. Everyone stands paused during the quiet standoff, and Merrill leans forward. He reaches out with a single finger and moves Quint's wet locks away from his face so that their opposing gazes connect. "You don't talk much, eh?" Quint continues his muted stare as Merrill continues. "I won't be as nice about it as my men are."

Quint jerks his head back and shakes his hair away from his face. He touches his tongue to a busted lip and rolls his jaw, as he looks around at the heavily-armed pirate crew on his sailboat deck. The air pirates are all silent as Merrill, with a contemplative stare, takes a step back and lets his unemotional scrutiny travel up into the ship's sail rigging. "Sir, do you have any idea who we might be or of the grave situation you are in?"

Testing his restraints, Quint flexes against the rope cord binding his wrists behind him. The provoked mariner hacks bloody spittle over the ship's railing and stares at his captor. "I know that I didn't give you permission to board my vessel, and I'm justified in shooting you the first chance I get."

Slightly entertained, the chief mate shakes his head and looks out to the overgrown island shore. Merrill puts his hands to his hips, and his jacket swings opens to reveal the grip handle of a German auto-pistol in an underarm holster. He glares down at Quint, speaking slowly and deliberately. "We already know you're not out here in the middle of nowhere on vacation. You transported a man and a woman to this island, and we are interested in what the woman has."

The sailor looks up at Merrill and smiles with bloody teeth. He shakes his head and lets out a sarcastic laugh. "I'm also interested in what women have."

A fist suddenly lashes out with a roundhouse punch, and Merrill knocks Quint and the chair backward to the deck. The chair topples to the wooden boards with a heavy thud. Merrill steps up to the prone mariner and hovers menacingly. "I am not interested in your jokes."

Quint blinks from the jolting punch and tumble back. He regains his breath and wriggles his tied wrists behind him, staring skyward. "What was it you were interested in again?"

Merrill kneels and gets face-to-face with Quint. His hot breath burns the bloody wound on Quint's forehead. "The man and the woman... Where are they?"

"Sorry fella, but I'm here by myself."

Dark pupils dancing with anger, Merrill clenches the muscles in his jaw, then his fists. A brief rustling in the underbrush on the island suddenly catches Merrill's attention. He draws his keen focus away from the intended victim and stands to face toward the nearby jungle. Three combat-attired pirates emerge from the vegetation, and one of them waves his machine gun over his head. Merrill moves to the aft rail of the sailboat to address the men. "What have you found?"

A tall, lean air-pirate steps forward and salutes feebly. "A fresh cut trail... Two people, traveling light."

Merrill smiles, satisfied, and glances back at Quint laid out on the deck. "Follow the trail and find them. Kill the man, but bring the woman back to me, preferably alive, along with any of her possessions." The three pirates snap a soldierly salute and disappear back into the jungle.

With slow leisurely footsteps, Merrill resumes his menacing stance over Quint. He casually blocks the bright sunshine from the fallen man's face, making it easier for him to look up at his captor. A perceptive smile moves over Merrill's hard features. "Have you a better story for me now?"

Quint gapes up at him blankly and then gives a reflexive squint, as Merrill pulls the sun-blocking shadow from over his eyes. There is a hushed silence on board the watercraft, as the two stare at each other. Quint offers a smirk before looking away.

Cross with the interrogation so far, and noticeably annoyed, Merrill delivers a swift kick to Quint's side. "No? Then I'll beat one out of you."

Merrill motions to two of the air pirates. They come over and lift Quint upright in the chair. Merrill waits patiently for an answer that doesn't come. He stares at Quint while the bound captive tugs against his ties and regains his breathing. The chief mate paces in front of Quint and then glances over toward the idle pirate seaplane and the open waters beyond.

"You could go free if you give me what I want. One way or another, I will get what I need from you."

Quint peeks up at him through an aching gasp of breath and spits. "Good luck. I got nothing to say."

Merrill smooths his hands down the front of his jacket and clenches his fists at his side. With hands hard as iron hammers, Merrill swings out and smashes his knuckles into Quint's face. The blow snaps Quint's head to the side and blood flows freely from his mouth, splashing to the deck. Merrill grabs Quint by his wet hair and turns his face to him. "We can do this the hard way…" He stares at the vulnerable captive fiercely, waiting for the answers that fail to come. Holding a handful of Quint's hair by the root in one hand, Merrill slams his other fist into his victim's exposed midsection. "…Or, we can do this the harder way."

Chapter 18

The midday sun turns the moist air over the lava-formed island into a tropical sauna. The humidity hangs heavy and glistens off the flowery hides of the spiders, as their legs cling to the heated steppingstones. Jimmy and Alexa cautiously climb the lava rock path toward the crescent moon-shaped opening near the top. Several spiders eyeball them warily before scurrying off.

The pair of explorers finally reaches a flat ledge just before the cave entrance, and Jimmy puts his hand out to stop Alexa from entering. "Hold it a minute."

"What is it?"

The temptation for discovery is powerful, as Alexa waits for Jimmy to peer into the darkness of the mountain cavity first. He turns around to face her, blocking the opening, and holds her tenderly by the shoulders. For a moment, Jimmy's gaze gets lost in her captivating emerald eyes, as intense feelings of longing well up inside him.

Alexa leans in closer to Jimmy, and at the heart-thumping moment he thinks they might kiss, she grimaces instead and peers inside the mountain cavity.

"We're going to need the flashlights," she whispers. She turns to the hired pilot and searches his face for a reply. "Are you okay, Jimmy?"

"Uh, yeah..."

"You look ill."

"I'm fine."

Jimmy breaks from his pining trance and looks at the multitude of large, colorful arachnids perched all over the surrounding rocks. "It's one thing to go dancing around toxic spiders outside where we can see 'em, but it's completely different crawling around with them in a dark cave."

Alexa grins wide and gives Jimmy a pecking kiss on the lips. "Stop worrying. According to the research, what we're looking for is in this cave, at the end of a passage. Come on... We're almost there. This is it!"

Alexa pulls two flashlights from the backpack and hands one to Jimmy. Her light clicks on, and she squeezes through the crevice. Jimmy turns to look out over the elevated view of the jungle island and shakes his head incredulously. "Suppose you just gave me the kiss of death."

Taking a deep breath, he clicks his flashlight on and follows her, through the narrow opening and into the mouth of the dark, rock mountain.

~*~

On the breezeless island coast, the air is still and heavy. Only the muted sounds of the jungle, blending in with the lap of tide water on the boat hull, can be heard. On the deck of the boat, a man's body lies on its side, still attached to a chair. Quint's face is a splattered mess of blood and bruising. The battered sailor breathes in light gasps, as he angles his face away from the sun. Blood flows from his nose and mouth, forming a small pool on the wooden surface.

Merrill leans back on the sail rigging and rubs his battered hands. His jacket is removed and small splotches of red stain his light-colored shirt and linen pants. The chief mate looks over at two of the pirate crew near the bow of the boat, playing dice. The small cubes clink and rattle as they continue their game of wager.

He stares awhile before looking to another pirate, sitting on the ship cabin rooftop, with the heavy Thompson machine gun cradled across his lap. Merrill continues rubbing his raw knuckles, on his fist, and looks down at his prisoner. With only faint gasps of audible breath, the beaten form lies motionless on the deck. Though his victim's eyes are closed, Merrill senses that Quint can feel his presence, and he notices the sailor trying to bury his pain.

The malicious interrogator walks over and slowly circles Quint again. The glare of the hot sun is intermittent, as Merrill's dark shadow passes over the prone body in the chair. The chief mate stops for a lingering moment and flexes his bloodied fingers. "It doesn't seem like we are getting anywhere. You continue to insist that you came here alone, even though I know you did not."

Taking a quick-step forward, Merrill delivers a swift kick to Quint's abdomen. He leans down closer, as the tied man gasps for air. "I am sorry for the interminable abuse, but I answer to someone not as forgiving as myself, who will find your mistruths and lack of information very tiring."

Coughing up bloody spit, Quint lets his eyes drift skyward while gulping desperately for a full breath of air. Merrill mercilessly bends down and grabs Quint's head by the hair. "It won't protect them any. They both will be recovered, and then I will have to kill you. You may even be looking forward to it."

Merrill sneers at the sailor's battered features and, with a heavy thud, drops Quint's head to the blood-smeared deck. He stands and walks away, leaving Quint to bake in the sun. Tilting his face away from the afternoon heat, Quint's wearied eyes roll back while his beaten body lies motionless in a pool of his own blood.

~*~

With machine guns at the ready, the heavily-armed air- pirates move at a hurried pace, following the path cut through the jungle. With the barrels of their rifles, they push the chopped and broken branches aside and duck under the hanging vines. Dressed like experienced, Second World War mercenaries, their mismatched uniforms create a strange unity amongst the group. Their military-style warfare boots make deep, distinct patterns in the soft, muddy ground.

The pirates move through a clearing and increase their pace to a trotting jog. One of the men stops before they re-enter the jungle and motions at the others to continue onward. In a thick, Polynesian accent, he shouts ahead to them. "Go on, I have to piss... I'll catch up." The others nod and quickly disappear into the greenery of the jungle.

The lingering pirate drops his automatic rifle to the ground and unfastens his trousers. A spurting spatter of urine soon trickles off the leafy ferns along the trail, and he turns his aim to a colorful spider lazing nearby. The confused creature dances in circles, as the pirate laughs uproariously while chasing it around with his stream.

"Run, run little spider..." Finished with his business, he watches the wet, confused creature dart off into the brush. He doesn't take notice as another eight-legged creature drops to his shoulder from an overhead tree-frond. The scratching of the large, probing legs on his neck alerts him to the spider's presence, and he tries to shake it off.

The pirate tucks himself away and fastens his trousers. He reaches to brush the eight-legged animal off of his neck, and it scurries across his back and onto the other shoulder. Swatting it away with his hand causes the spider to suddenly tense up and bite down, through the thin cloth shirt, into the fleshy part of his shoulder.

Horrified, the man yelps in pain and rips the furry assailant from his shoulder. He throws it to the ground, next to his machine gun and quickly smashes it with his boot heel. He uses his shirt sleeve as a daubing bandage, wincing as he gingerly touches around the open wound.

The air pirate takes a deep, strained breath and reaches down to pick up his automatic-rifle. His eyes go wide with shock, as a pulse of blinding pain shoots through his body. With blurred vision, he looks down to see that there is another spider attached to his leg. He draws his knife blade and slashes at the spider, gouging deep into his own calf muscle.

Another spider skitters from the underbrush, and he quickly stabs at that one as well. He jerks violently, as another bite painfully surges through his body. Spiders aggressively scurry from the foliage and drop from the trees, as the man falls to the ground, convulsing in a flowery bouquet of arachnids.

The first of the air pirates emerge from the thick jungle vegetation and discover the zig-zagged pathway up the large, mountainous pile of rocks. They briefly see the glimmer of flashlights in the cavernous gap near the top of the mound. With shrewd smiles, the two pirates turn to each other and proceed to climb upward.

Chapter 19

On the inside of the mountain peak cavern, Jimmy and Alexa shine their flashlights around at the walls of the surprisingly large cavity. At the far end of the space, the lit beams reveal two dark passages. Jimmy looks to Alexa questioningly. "What does your journal say now?"

"It doesn't." Using the light, she looks at her book while shaking her head.

Jimmy snorts cynically. "I thought you did your homework?"

"It has to be one or the other."

Jimmy leans further over her shoulder and tries to read the scribbles. "Is that what you wrote in there?"

She shrugs, as she carefully studies the written notations. "This message roughly translates to, *Follow the righteous path, else death will shortly follow.*"

As their flashlights shine on the two separate routes, they both remain quiet. Alexa looks at Jimmy as he silently stares, and asks, "Well, what do you think?"

"I think it's a sick joke."

"Me too." Alexa moves ahead and, collectively, they dread the choice between the two dark passages before them.

~*~

The tethered sailboat remains in the calm, rising tide-waters as it seems to slowly distance itself from the shore. Merrill sits near the unmanned helm and quietly looks out to the jungle as he waits. Impatient for the return of his hunting party, he looks to Quint, laid out on the deck. He then marches toward the pirates at the bow of the ship, still engaged in their game of dice.

When the chief mate approaches, they quickly hold the roll and wait for his command. As he fixes his stare on the pirate with the numbered cubes in hand, Merrill tilts his head toward the rear section of the sailboat. "Move to the helm and be on the lookout for any sign of our men and their prize."

Obedient, the pirate quickly pockets the dice and grabs his Thompson machine gun. The other pirate crewmember stands up, gun in hand, and Merrill nods toward the dingy. "You, take me to the air-ship. I need to establish radio contact with Captain Rasmus."

~*~

The ancient cave is cool and moist, as Jimmy and Alexa cautiously use a narrow, muddy pathway as they make their way down one of the passages. The two flashlight beams extend several meters ahead before fading into the darkness. The damp, musty air fills their lungs, making them both breathe heavily. Alexa shines the light at her feet, as she coughs from the stale air. "How far do you think this goes?"

"This mountain isn't all that large. It seems like we've been sloping down a ways though... It won't be long until we reach the waterline."

Despite the slick mud on the floor, they continue moving downward while shining their beams of light ahead. Jimmy reaches out to the side and touches the wetness of the cool, stone wall. "At least there aren't any spiders in here."

Alexa's footing slips in the mud and Jimmy catches her. She looks up at him, gratefully, through the dim light.

"Yeah, that's a relief."

~*~

At the crescent-shaped entrance to the mountain cave, the air pirates squeeze through the fissure and stand silhouetted in the opening. The one pirate looks to the other. "You have a flashlight?"

"No, do you?"

The first pirate pulls a small, finger-sized flashlight from his vest pocket and clicks it on. He shines the tiny beam across the cavern toward the passageways at the opposite end. "You want to wait for them here?"

The second pirate flicks open his Zippo lighter and gives it a scratch. The flame illuminates his unpleasantness and he smiles wicked. "They can't be far. Let's go get 'em."

They move through the cave toward the passageways. The pirate with the penlight shines the narrow beam a few feet into each tunnel. "You take that one and I'll take this one. Do whatever it takes with the man, but bring the woman." Smiling, they both duck into separate passages and disappear into the blackness.

~*~

The twin beams from the flashlights reveal that the dark, muddy passageway is becoming noticeably steeper. Jimmy and Alexa hold onto the smooth walls, trying to keep from sliding forward. While holding the flashlight pointed at the mud-slicked floor, Alexa eases herself slowly down. Jimmy follows behind and peers ahead into the dark tunnel. "Step careful. We should be nearing the water level anytime now. There's no telling if the rising tide will come up sudden and wash us out."

Alexa shines her light ahead and stares into the void. "It could do that?"

Jimmy shrugs, unsure. "Who knows...? We're in the middle of a volcanic tube on an uncharted island surrounded by ocean... And we're walking deeper and deeper inside it." His footing slips on the steep tunnel floor, and he quickly recovers, looking ahead to see Alexa braced in front of him. "There might be a pressure valve below where the water rushes in all at once. Quint mentioned that we were at the beginning of a rising tide. These floors are wet for a reason."

Alexa looks back, directly into Jimmy's flashlight beam. "Well, let's hurry then."

They warily slide down a few feet of the wet corridor. Alexa suddenly loses her footing completely, falling and slipping down the passageway. She quickly drops from sight, as she glides around a corner and disappears into the darkness. Jimmy skids down the tunnel, bracing himself against the walls. "Alexa…!"

Jimmy retains his grip on the flashlight while holding onto the slick stone walls and carefully sliding forward. Suddenly, he takes a misstep, and his feet skate as if on ice. Grasping at the smooth tunnel sides for a handhold, Jimmy falls and quickly disappears down the sloping passageway.

~*~

Alexa shoots blindly down the muddy luge and slides into a pool of water, followed shortly after by her flashlight. Illuminated by a slender shaft of daylight from far above, she stands in the waist-deep water and frantically looks around. In the quiet dimness, she reaches down to her feet and retrieves her flashlight, when she suddenly hears Jimmy tumbling down.

"Son of a…"

Ungracefully, Jimmy shoots out from the opening of the tunnel and splashes across the surface of the pool of water. Finding his way, Jimmy stands, flustered and soaking wet. Alexa shines her flashlight at him and laughs. He stares at her grimly and replies, "You think this is funny?"

"A little…"

Jimmy grips his flashlight tightly and wades back toward the passageway. He shines it upward and peers into the emptiness. "You won't think it so amusing when we try to get back out that way."

Alexa shines her light around the cavern. Her light stops at a small opening, high over the opposite end of the shallow pool.

"Let's get out that way."

Jimmy wipes the water from his face and pushes his wet hair back. "Has it even occurred to you that we might have chosen the wrong path?"

She wades toward the far side of the cavern and looks back over her shoulder at Jimmy splashing along behind her. "Yes. It has crossed my mind. Now, let's go." Alexa suddenly drops from view under the water and Jimmy reaches down and pulls her to the surface. She sputters a mouthful of seawater and smiles meekly. "There's a bit of a drop off."

Jimmy licks his lips and spits. "It's salt water."

"So?"

He shines his light all around the grotto walls. "This is a tide pool. In a few hours, this place will be full of water... Probably the corridors too."

"No time to waste then."

"Are you kidding me?"

"Until we're in real danger, I'm not leaving without it." She dives forward and starts to swim toward the opposite wall, as Jimmy reluctantly follows.

~*~

Just off the island coast, inside the pirate Catalina seaplane, Merrill stands at the door to the cockpit and listens to the radio hum with electricity. The crewman operating the transmitter adjusts the frequency and clicks the receiver. "Calling Catalina P. M. R., this is A. P. Two-Twenty, do you copy?"

The static continues, and Merrill slams his palm on the steel-riveted wall. The chief mate's impatient slap on the bulkhead startles the radio operator, and he adjusts the dials. Merrill looks past the radio station, out the windows to the anchored sailboat across the water, and clenches his jaw tight. "Keep trying on each channel. As soon as you make contact, let me know immediately."

"Yes, sir."

The radio operator pulls his headphones over both ears and adjusts the radio frequencies again. Irritated, Merrill turns and disappears from the oval-shaped doorway of the cockpit. The pirate seaplane heaves gently in the ocean swells, as empty radio static echoes inside the headphones.

Chapter 20

After scaling the wet stone wall, Alexa climbs through the small opening near the top of the cavern. Her flashlight beam flits around the inside hollow of the tunnel entrance. Highlighted by the bright light in hand, Alexa pokes her head out and looks down at Jimmy still climbing behind her. "C'mon, Captain Ferral."

He grunts, as he tries to secure a foothold on the stone. "What's up there? Did you find it?"

"Looks like another short passageway."

Jimmy slips on the wall, but manages to hang on. Perturbed, he glances up at her. "What do you mean *short*? The last one dropped us below the waterline."

"C'mon, Jimmy, you're wasting time."

As he continues to climb from the tide pool, Jimmy grumbles obscenities to himself. The brightness from Alexa's flashlight illuminates the outer ledge of the opening and Jimmy finally gets a handhold and pulls up. He crawls inside, clicks on his own light, and shines it down the corridor, illuminating another seemingly endless path. "Now what?"

Alexa opens her backpack and wipes the moisture off the cover of her leather-bound journal. She scrolls her light down the damp-edged pages, flips a few, finally shining her beam at the last scribbled passage. "On to the treasure."

"It doesn't say a damn thing, does it?"

He leans over to read her treasure journal, and she snaps it closed before he can catch a glimpse. She half smiles and ushers him forward down the dark path. "Let's go."

Jimmy returns her prodding with an insincere smile and bows with a gesture for her to proceed. "No, I insist... After you, Madam"

Alexa moves ahead and leads the way up the slightly inclined passageway.

~*~

In the muddy cave tunnel, an air pirate works his way slowly down the sloped corridor. He shines his small flashlight on the path before him and suddenly slips forward. Holding his rifle and grasping at the walls, he fumbles with his light and hastily falls down the slope and into darkness.

With a sliding swoosh, the pirate crashes into the tide pool below. He pops up from the slowly rising water, clutching his machine gun with both hands. He looks around at the dark cavern and into the murky water. Then, the pirate looks to the faint source of flashlight beams coming from above and listens.

~*~

A splash of water echoes in the cavern behind, and Jimmy turns to shine his flashlight down the passageway from where they just came. He stands quietly for a moment and strains to hear any sounds in the dark tunnel. Alexa pivots on her heel and shines her light at him. "What is it?"

"*Shh...* I thought I heard something."

They both look behind, down the narrow path, and shine their flashlights toward the empty chamber beyond. Listening intently, they wait at the edge of the darkness. Jimmy clicks off his light and pushes Alexa's lamp beam down toward their feet. He holds his breath for a moment and then shakes his head. "I don't know. Could be just the water rising with the coming tide. Let's keep moving." Jimmy clicks his light back on again and shines it one more time down the empty corridor.

~*~

The pirate stands motionless in the chest-deep tide pool, as he watches the shafts of light disappear from the opening on the opposite wall. The darkness returns and he bumps his small flashlight floating at the surface and grabs it. With his machine gun slung over his shoulder, he swims across to the far side of the pool and easily climbs to the upper passageway above the ever-rising water.

~*~

The pair breathe heavily, as they hike through the tight, dank tunnel. Noticing a change in the ground consistency, Jimmy stops Alexa. "Hold up here for a bit." He bends down to examine the path ahead.

"Why? Is your shoe untied?"

Sneering at her smart-ass comment, Jimmy glances at her and lifts a loose stick from the stone floor. He wags it at her and asks, curiously, "Why are there dead branches in here?"

Alexa shrugs and shines her flashlight around their feet. "Maybe the tide pool washed them in?"

Using the stick as a probing guide, Jimmy moves past Alexa and he pokes the ground ahead of them. "From where? Trees grow above the land, not under it."

She shrugs. "I'm an archeologist, not an arborist."

Jimmy takes the lead and Alexa follows him, watching as he jabs the stick into the branch-scattered ground a bit farther up the corridor. The brush-covered floor suddenly drops out, exposing a gaping hole in the path. Cautiously stepping to the rim of the abyss, they shine their flashlights into the void. The shafts of light reveal pikes, with sharpened points, meant to impale an unsuspecting victim, protruding from the walls and base of the pit. Jimmy glances up at Alexa and grimaces. "That's why you pay me, Madam."

"I wish you'd stop calling me that."

"Whatever you say, Boss-lady."

Keeping close to the wall, they ease their way around the uninviting pit and point their flashlights up the steadily inclining path. Jimmy trips slightly and notices several steps are notched into the ascending rock. "It's all uphill from here. Would you like to lead?"

Alexa smiles warily. "Uh, no thanks, Captain. You're doing a wonderful job."

"That's what I figured." Jimmy cynically rolls his eyes, shines the flashlight ahead, and takes the first step up the primitive stone stairway.

~*~

The afternoon sun shines down on the wooden sailboat, nodding on the sea swells just off the rocky shore. Mid-deck, Quint lays face down, limp and immobile, but still firmly tied to the chair. With dried and crusted blood on his clothes, he moans slightly and continues to take in shallow breaths.

Sitting nearby, with a machine gun laid across his lap, an air pirate relaxes in the shade of the sail-wrapped mast. The pirate scans the thick, jungle coastline. The sounds of the island wildlife chatters in a muted tone from the underbrush and birds occasionally flutter from the treetops.

~*~

Jimmy and Alexa move through the dark corridor and enter another cavern, larger than the first. They step into the open cavity, moving through it until Jimmy shines his light down at their feet where the floor seems to come to an end. Extending an arm to stop Alexa from advancing, he aims the handheld light forward and the beam fades into blackness.

"This is it. We chose the wrong path."

Alexa shines her flashlight around the cave and sniffs. "Do you smell fire?"

Jimmy breathes the smoke-tinged, musty air, as he peers past the toes of his boots over the brink into the dark, seemingly endless abyss below. "A little... That's strange." Curious, Jimmy steps back from the ledge, and scans his light over the stone floor. He stops at a burned piece of cloth wrapped on a stick—a makeshift torch—still smoking. "Alexa...?"

As she turns, the click and scratch of a Zippo lighter illuminates the features of a lurking pirate pressed against the wall behind Jimmy. She screams and drops her flashlight, which clanks, flickers, and goes rolling, across the floor. Spinning with his own beam of light, Jimmy stands nearly face-to-face with the second air pirate.

Before Jimmy can react and draw his pistol, the waiting pirate swings the barrel of his rifle, knocking him to the floor. The air pirate holds his automatic rifle in one hand, clicks his lighter closed, and grabs Jimmy's flashlight from the ground. He aims the light and rifle at Alexa and looks down to Jimmy. "Eh, fella, leave your gun on the ground."

Jimmy releases the ready firearm from his grip. The cold metal clatters on the stone floor, and Jimmy holds out his open hands. The pirate shines the flashlight in Alexa's face and motions her toward the ledge.

"Both of you get over there."

Jimmy stares down at the discarded weapon on the cave floor and is almost tempted to reach for it. As he stands and walks the short distance to Alexa, he notices the second passageway entrance into the room. The pirate follows his inquisitive gaze and steps in front of the opening. He raises his rifle to his shoulder and points it threateningly. "That was easy enough. Now, what is this I hear about a treasure?"

Forcing a smile to hide her fear, Alexa shakes her head. "We don't have any treasure."

Returning the intrepid smile, the air pirate shines the flashlight over to an old twisted rope anchored to the wall. They watch as the lighted beam slowly traces the horizontal length of ragged, jungle-weaved vines across the void. Redirecting the shaft of light, the pirate illuminates a niche on the opposite wall.

Across the dark abyss, on a narrow rock ledge, sits an aged, human skull encased in taut, dried skin. Atop its sparse strands of wispy white hair rests a jeweled headpiece that glimmers faintly in the diffused light. Flashing a malicious and toothy smirk, the pirate comments, "Is that what everyone is looking for? Now, go and get it."

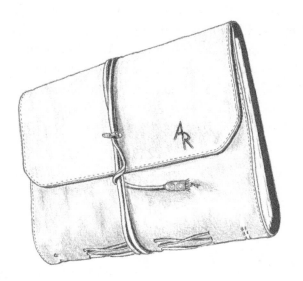

Chapter 21

The cave is now illuminated by wood-handled torches stuck in cradles cut into the stone walls by native people long ago. Flickering, bright orange firelight fills the room and casts shadows into the dark corners. Jimmy stands near the ancient hand-twisted rope stretched across the chasm, and he gives it a tug to test its durability.

Alexa watches nervously. "Will that hold you?"

Jimmy looks at her and puts on a smirking grin. "They sure don't make things like they used to." He pulls heavily on the thick rope, with his full weight. The aged, woven twine creaks and groans as if it might give out at any moment. He turns to the air pirate standing near the corridor opening, blocking their escape.

The pirate keeps the automatic rifle pointed at them and gestures him onward. "Go ahead."

Jimmy shakes his head. "This thing won't support me. Who knows how old it is?"

Alexa clears her throat. "A hundred years old."

The pilot turns his face to her and frowns sarcastically. "Thank you for the facts, professor."

The pirate takes several steps forward and pokes Jimmy hard with the muzzle of his machine gun. He glances over at the distant treasure on the opposite wall and smiles. "Try it. Or send her instead."

Jimmy and Alexa exchange a heartfelt regard, before he reaches for the aged rope again. Small fibers break free, as he pulls himself up and swings his feet over the creaking strands. Moving backward toward the treasure, reaching hand over hand, Jimmy works his way across the open abyss. Alexa crosses her arms on her chest, anxiously hugging herself. "Be careful."

Jimmy looks back at her and then down at the void below. "Thanks... Be right back."

~*~

The afternoon shadows of the taller jungle trees on the island lengthen, stretching out toward the tethered sailboat. Merrill marches across the foredeck, watching for any movement inside the darkening jungle. The chatter of insects and an occasional bird call emanates from the twisted foliage.

He looks down at Quint and squats next to the bound captive fastened to the fallen chair. Merrill watches the slow, measured breaths of the battered mariner and sighs irritably. He turns Quint's head and holds him by the scalp as he studies the blood-crusted interrogee. "It's getting late. Where are your friends?"

Quint opens a swollen eye. "Where are yours?"

The chief mate's jaw clenches, and he drops Quint's head to the blood-stained planks of the deck.

Merrill stands upright, wipes his messed hand on the gathered folds of the mainsail and stares again to the jungle. He shakes his head and steps away, seething with frustration.

~*~

The glow of firelight inside of the cave begins to fade as the primitive torches burn away and disintegrate. Jimmy continues to work his way across the dimly lit cavern on the ancient, sagging rope. As he nears the ledge, the twist of organic twine gives a creaking groan and several strands snap with a *popping* sound. Jimmy holds his breath as he drops a few inches and dangles closer to the rock outcropping. "Ohh, damn…"

Watching impatiently, the pirate shines the flashlight toward the ledge holding the headpiece, as Jimmy swings down to relative safety. They watch as Jimmy cautiously lifts the crown from the ancient skull and examines it carefully. With the exception of the precious stones, the headpiece is rather dull and tarnished. Jimmy rubs it with his thumb to reveal a golden shimmer underneath. "Could use a cleaning."

Gurgling water echoes through the cavern and the pirate shines the flashlight back at the passage where he planned to make his retreat. The entrance at the bottom of the cave slowly fills with water. Just a few inches roll in at first, followed by a steadily rising tide.

The sharp echo of gunfire, a blinding muzzle flash and bullets ricocheting off the stone walls, shakes Jimmy from his infatuated study of the treasure. He turns to see the pirate holding a smoking automatic rifle in one hand and clutching Alexa by the shirt collar with the other. The ill-humored treasure poacher cradles the flashlight under his arm and, with his gun, motions to Jimmy. "That's enough time-wasting. Toss it over here!"

The pirate looks over his shoulder again at the water level steadily rising in the lower corridor exit. "Hurry it up, before the passage fills with water."

Jimmy looks down at the valuable headpiece and, with an amused smirk, back at the pirate. He reaches out and hangs one hand on the creaking rope overhead.

"You want me to toss it over? Are you kidding?"

As the pirate raises the rifle at Jimmy, the flashlight under his arm falls to the floor and rolls aside.

"How about I kill you now?"

"And lose your big reward for finding the treasure? You'll just have to wait until I get across, before you kill us.

Alexa looks from Jimmy to the barrel of the still-smoking machine gun. "That's a great plan, Jimmy."

The pirate squeezes off a few more bursts of ammo rounds that slam into the rock wall, sending splinters of stone cascading down over Jimmy. The deafening echo and blinding flash from the firearm's muzzle strains everyone's senses. "Who said anything about killing her? Now bring it over."

Jimmy lashes the headpiece to his waist belt with an old piece of fabric near the skull and grabs the rope overhead. Slowly, he swings up and begins the arduous task of the return traverse. The pirate looks down at the lower passage, anxiously watching as it continues to fill with the rising water. He turns to Jimmy, still mid-rope, but slowly scooting closer. "Quicker, damn you!"

"I am..." Several more strands of the twisted rope snap, bouncing Jimmy's feet from the line. In the flashlight beam, shining across the floor, a haze of ancient rope particles float and drift in the musty air. Jimmy hangs by one arm, midway across the dark abyss.

Alexa jumps forward and screams. "Jimmy!!"

The pirate shoves her aside and takes his eye off them both for a moment, as he bends down to pick up the flashlight. Jimmy holds on the old rope and, with a quick sleight of hand, reaches into his front pocket to pull out his flip-blade knife. The pirate shines the light on Jimmy as he hangs, mid-rope, and urges him closer. With feet still dangling, Jimmy reaches up and grabs the rope with both hands and smiles at Alexa.

"I know honey... Don't drop the headpiece."

Hand over hand, Jimmy begins to work his way back. As he nears the shelf of rock where Alexa and the pirate wait, he slips the knife blade between the woven fibers of rope. Several of the fragile strands break free and Jimmy firms his forward grip tighter as he heaves his weight, making the rope line bounce slightly. Suddenly, the entire rope gives out and, for an instant, Jimmy is suspended mid-air before dropping into the empty abyss.

Alexa dashes forward and peers over the shadowy edge, trying to catch sight of him. "Ohhh, Jimmy... Jimmy!" She scans the dark void and then the stretched line that drops over the brink. Groans can be heard at the end of the ancient rope, as it twitches from the efforts of someone climbing.

"I'm still here."

The pirate steps forward and cautiously leans out to look over the rim. He stares into the empty darkness and steps back from the edge of the chasm. "We don't have time for this. Do you still have the treasure?"

There is a silent pause as the pirate turns from the rope, where it drops over the ledge, to the water-filled passageway behind him. Angry, the pirate yells again. "Do you have it?"

The rope twists as Jimmy renews the task of climbing. "It dropped from my belt."

Alexa peers over the side and gasps. "How could you! Are you sure?"

Confusion and panic cross the pirate's features, as he shakes his head in disbelief and looks back to the corridor, nearly filled with water. "You dropped the treasure, you say?"

A strained voice is heard from below. "It's gone."

The pirate pushes Alexa aside, unsheathes his knife, and starts to slash at the rope's attachment on the wall. Alexa gapes in horror, as the pirate keeps his rifle aimed at her and attempts to cut the remaining strands.

"What are you doing?"

"Step back! We don't need him anymore."

The final strands of twine snap and the rope separates from the wall. Alexa grabs for the cut line, but it only slips through her fingers and disappears over the rocky brink. Alexa cries in horror, as the twisted vine vanishes into the quiet abyss, "No... Jimmy!!!"

The air pirate snatches her by the arm and pulls her toward the lower exit he arrived through. They stop short and watch as the last few inches of the passageway fill with water. The pirate turns Alexa to the other tunnel and pushes her toward it. "Quickly, show me the path you took."

He aims the flashlight back toward the ledge where the rope slid over into nothingness and waits for any signs of life. Alexa holds back her tears, as the light shines across into the darkness. "I'm so sorry, Jimmy…"

The pirate pushes her violently toward the opening and she accidentally kicks her fallen flashlight across the hard, stone floor. The metallic tube rolls, blinks, and turns out. Alexa trips to the ground, drops her pack from her shoulder, and holds both her arms out to protect herself from the pirate. He gives a swift kick to her leg and growls, "You better keep being of use, or I'll kill you too. Show me the way out."

Grabbing her by the back of the neck, the pirate shoves Alexa toward the remaining accessible passageway, and they quickly duck inside.

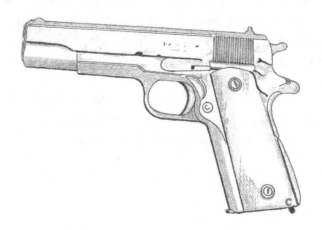

Chapter 22

The Air Pirate travels quickly through the damp corridor, shining the light ahead and pulling Alexa along behind. They move down the stone carved stairs and stumble in the broken darkness on the frond-scattered floor when they reach the last of the descending steps. They both stop abruptly when the flashlight illumination comes to a gaping hole in the path.

The flashlight in the pirate's hand tips downward into the dark hole to reveal the other air pirate gruesomely impaled by several sharpened poles near the bottom of the pit. Alexa pulls back and turns away, repulsed by the sight. In a foreign tongue, the somber pirate murmurs under his breath. "Goodbye, my friend."

Alexa tries to bolt away, but her captor keeps his grip. "Hold it there, girlie! You could easily join him right now." The pirate pulls her close, then thrusts her forcefully out over the edge of the pit. With her feet still at the rim, Alexa dangles precariously over the deadly precipice. She turns her head away and falls back into the pirate's firm hold. They both ease around the void and cautiously travel farther down the passageway.

~*~

The only sound in the cavern is the crackle of fire. The burning embers from the fiery torches, stuck in the wall, float to the stone floor and slowly fade out. The cave is bathed in a darkening glow of dying flames.

At the edge of the cavern, across the abyss from the former resting place of the treasure, a tenacious hand reaches over the stone rim. His climbing grasp is followed by heavy breaths and panting grunts. The other hand reaches up, and Jimmy's head peeks over.

The glow of dying torches flash and flicker across Jimmy's features, as he rises, head and shoulders, above the chasm. He looks around the empty cave as his eyes adjust to the faint light. His cautious gaze comes to rest on his pistol, where it lies on the ground, and Alexa's pack near the wall. Jimmy heaves a sigh of temporary relief, as a hint of a grin curls at the edges of his mouth. He puts his elbows on the ledge and completes his struggle up.

~*~

At the cavernous tide pool, dim rays of daylight stream in from far overhead. The pirate and his captive arrive at the tunnel intersection and look out over the rising water level. Alexa looks down to see that it has risen nearly to their feet.

The air pirate shines his flashlight around the grotto and halts his beam directly on the passage opening opposite to them. The water has moved to within inches of covering the tunnel. "Is that the way?"

Alexa feigns unfamiliarity and looks back at the tunnel they just came from. "We must have taken a wrong turn."

"What turn?"

"Back there a-ways."

When the pirate peers over his shoulder, Alexa snatches the flashlight from him and slams her fist to the side of his cheek. Alexa clicks off the light and dives into the pool. Her entry splash settles, and the water laps quietly as she swims underwater toward the tunnel exit.

Momentarily raising her head above the dark, tide pool to take a breath, she hears the pirate splash in behind her. Alexa ducks down again and kicks toward the passageway tunnel, now underwater. Probing the submerged stone wall, Alexa briefly clicks on the flashlight to help her to locate the water-blocked exit.

Inside the flooded passage leading from the tide pool, Alexa holds her breath and feels her way through the pitch-dark tunnel. She swims several yards before she is able to raise her head above the water and gasp for air. Holding onto the walls with great physical exertion, Alexa pulls herself along the slick muddy floor. Finally she stands and jogs toward the main entrance of the dormant volcanic cave.

Alexa collapses at the mouth of the cavern and lies in a warm swath of late afternoon sunlight. Without her backpack and soaking wet, she heaves her lungs, gasping for breath. Alexa looks to the cave exit, as she pushes her dripping-wet hair back from her face.

Outside the cave, the last remaining hours of daylight can be seen colorfully tinged on the clouds as the sky darkens. She stares blankly, feeling an aching pang of remorse at the loss of her brazen seaplane pilot. Finally climbing to her feet, she feels a sharp stabbing pain from the gun barrel of an automatic rifle being jabbed into her back. She turns to see a sopping wet, furiously irate, air pirate.

"That wasn't a nice thing to do." The foul-breathed pirate licks his bloodied lip and sneers.

~*~

The sound of boots echoes in the empty stone corridor. A dark form heaves for a breath of air and stops at the edge of the glimmering tide pool. The clank of metal against metal is heard as the butt of a handgun taps a flashlight and the beam blinks on. Jimmy's boots splash in a puddle, as he looks down at the water coming up into the passageway.

He stands in an inch of rising seawater and, looking for the passage exit, scans his flashlight along the opposite wall. All but covered with the rising tide, the tunnel reveals itself as a stream of bubbles gurgle up from the opening. He shakes his head and shines the light around the flooding grotto in a last effort to search for an alternate route of escape. "Ahh, damn it! I told her it wouldn't be easy…"

Tucking his pistol into Alexa's canvas backpack, Jimmy tightens the closing leather straps, clicks off the flashlight, and dives into the rising tide pool with a plopping splash.

Chapter 23

"Get your hands off me!" Alexa is violently shoved through the cave's crescent opening, as the air pirate follows behind.

He growls, "Get going. I want to be back by nightfall." Alexa takes a faltered step and the pirate reaches out, grabs her face and turns her head forcibly before leaning in close. "Get moving, or I'll deal you the same favor you did for me." Tripping backward, she nearly falls down the steep rocks, but the pirate catches her. "You won't get away so easily again." He laughs as he holds her upper arm snug and pushes her down the path toward the jungle below. Alexa turns to face the air pirate and tries to muster some semblance of authority. "I can pay you to let me go."

Her abductor stops and smiles. "Let you go? Your friend with the sailboat is probably already dead."

The color drains from Alexa's features, as she is hustled forward down the rock pathway. Remorsefully, she thinks of Quint and Jimmy being casualties of her mission. A feeling of dread washes over her, as she senses that her imprisonment by Captain Rasmus and his pirate crew is close at hand.

~*~

Jimmy explodes from the dark, flooded passage and gasps for air. He clicks on the flashlight and shines it ahead. Wading through the chest-deep water, Jimmy pushes toward higher ground. He moves farther up the water-filled corridor, and the depth lessens. Bracing himself on the slick walls, he slogs and splashes through the wet tunnel.

In the damp corridor, Jimmy slips Alexa's backpack from his shoulders, and he takes out his pistol. Sliding the canvas rucksack back onto his shoulders, he proceeds onward with the gun in one hand and flickering flashlight in the other. Shining the beam ahead, he moves quickly but cautiously toward the exit of the cavern.

~*~

Steadily moving along, Alexa and the air pirate continue to climb down the steep, boulder-strewn path. With constant prodding from the barrel of the pirate's machine gun, Alexa barely has a moment's pause to contemplate an escape. He pushes her forward, kicks a flowery spider from his path and looks out to the dense jungle ahead. "Keep moving."

The pirate jabs her again with the weapon's sharp gunsight and, she collapses to the ground in a wet, breathless jumble of emotions. "I need to rest."

"You get up now, or you won't ever again."

Alexa shakes her head at the menacing presence above her and peers up, exhausted. He glares at her and slides his finger over the machine gun's trigger. After several gestures with the tip of the barrel, she slowly makes a move to rise.

Standing before the pirate, Alexa regains her poise and stumbles down the path to the dense tropical forest below. Crossing the path between them, a large flower-like spider momentarily distracts the pirate. He halts and briefly assesses his surroundings before following after his captive.

~*~

A flash of light cuts through the darkness and emerges from the passageway to the entry cavern. With his gun at the ready, Jimmy guardedly shines his beam around the hollow, stone room. He carefully moves over to the other passage entrance and momentarily shines his light into the black void.

Turning the aim of his light to the cave floor, he follows the sets of wet footprints that trail upward to the entryway. Cautiously, he pokes his head out of the cave entrance, blinking in the afternoon sunlight. He looks out to the trail below and watches, as the pirate pushes Alexa to the beginning of the jungle path.

"Jeez Alexa, slow down… What's your hurry?"

With the canvas backpack still on his shoulders, Jimmy slides through the crevice and begins to work his way down the rocky descent to the jungle below.

~*~

The sound of wildlife chatters and echoes in the trees as the pair maneuver their way along the freshly blazed trail. Alexa is pushed ahead by the gun-toting air pirate following close behind her. She swipes aside the partially severed branches that hang limp in her path. Despite the weeping wounds of recently hacked foliage, the jungle has begun to restore itself and seems to close in over the scarred path.

Alexa stops a moment, dabs sweat from her brow and glances back at the pirate. She looks down to the long knife on his belt. "It would be faster going if I had that blade to chop my way through here."

The pirate looks down at the knife blade at his side and looks up at her with a wicked grin. "You'd like to sink my steel into something, eh missy?"

He raises his machine gun and motions Alexa forward. The pair continues trekking through the thick, jungle brush. She pushes a low-hanging palm leaf aside, revealing a small clearing in the surrounding foliage and steps forward. Suddenly, Alexa jumps back and gasps, as she stares down at a dead figure, grotesquely swollen, lying prone on the ground. "Uh, do you know him?"

Shoving Alexa aside, the pirate leans down and turns the dead man over. The deceased pirate's bloated, purple features are pocked with bloody gouges, oozing a vile yellow pus-like substance.

"How in the hell?"

He drops to both knees in grief and lays his automatic rifle across his lap. He stares at his dead friend for a while, and then turns to look up at Alexa. "What sort of animal could've done this?"

Alexa offers an innocent shrug as she glances to the many colorful arachnids ostensibly watching them from the surrounding greenery. While the pirate gawps down at his fallen comrade, Alexa delivers a roundhouse kick to his head that tumbles him over the swollen corpse. Dashing away, Alexa lunges into the thick, untamed jungle.

Clinging vines and branches grab at Alexa's legs, causing her to stumble and trip as she runs. She flees through the underbrush, while razor-sharp palm fronds cut at her arms and face. A short distance in, she pauses and hears the sounds of a body crashing through the jungle behind and the cursing of the pirate in pursuit.

Alexa keeps going, unsure of which direction to head. Suddenly, her feet stop moving and, as she grabs for something to hold to, she tumbles forward into a pool of mud. Frantically, she tries to put her feet down on something firm, but she only succeeds in working her way deeper into the sludge. As Alexa squirms to cross the quagmire, the air pirate runs into the bog, splashing up mud as he enters.

The pirate's machine gun lands with a plop just beyond his reach, and he paddles toward it while sinking deeper. Unable to reach the gun floating on the surface of the muck, he begins to thrash in serious panic. Alexa calls out to him, "Struggling only makes it worse."

The pirate glares at her, enraged, and turns his grasping reach toward her. She lies back with her arms spread wide, attempting to delay her descent.

Clawing his way toward her, the air pirate slowly sinks deeper and deeper. His mouth starts to dip below the surface, and he coughs through the mud, gasping for air. With a gurgling sound that bubbles up from the swampy pond, his face slowly sinks under the surface. Alexa turns away, as only his arm pokes above the muck, clutching for life.

Alexa tries to move through the thick quagmire. She grabs for a dangling jungle vine, just beyond her outstretched fingertips and sinks a little deeper. "Uh, help?" A bird flutters to a nearby tree as she looks around, powerless. "Help!" Alexa remains stationary and continues to slowly sink in the swampy pit.

~*~

The shadows from the jungle trees cast a cooling shade over the warm lava rocks leading down from the mountain. Jimmy climbs down the boulder path, exhausted and wary. The oversized, flowery spiders begin to move and scurry around, hunting for an evening meal.

Carefully stepping around the poisonous creatures, Jimmy maneuvers his way to the bottom of the rock-strewn path. He scans the area, and then studies the rough-cut trail through the vegetation, noticing the prominent boot tracks going both directions. Wiping the sweat from his face, he plunges into the jungle.

~*~

The swamp of mud settles as Alexa sinks deeper into the pit until only to have her head and arms protruding out. She tries not to look at the clenched hand of the pirate, a few feet away, dangling lifeless in the mud. Turning her head, trying not to move her body,

Alexa hears a familiar chatter. "Curtiss? Oh, my friend Curtiss, is that you?"

The leaves of the jungle rustle and the monkey copilot's hairy toes appear at the edge of the swampy pit. He peeks out and displays a toothy grin at Alexa, neck-deep in the mire.

"Stay there, Curtiss. Don't come over here."

Confused, the monkey crawls forward and tests the squishy ground gingerly with his open palm.

"Something to grab… Something to hold on to."

Questioningly, Curtiss reaches up and yanks on an overhanging tree limb. He pulls it downward, raking the mud, but still out of Alexa's limited reach.

"That's a good boy! Something like that!"

Curtiss climbs into the tree and attempts to pull vines loose from the tangled foliage.

The afternoon sun slants through the trees overhead and the jungle air remains thick and humid. Alexa watches her furry friend tug on tree creepers, while a fat, colorful spider delicately walks across the surface of the muddy pit. She notices the eight-legged beast look around curiously before continuing on. Trying not to squirm, Alexa eyes the noxious spider and holds her breath until it scurries away, into the greenery.

"Hurry Curtiss!"

The monkey stops his work and turns to her with canted head, as she murmurs, "Please…"

With a jerk, Curtiss finally frees a leafy vine and swings to the ground near Alexa. The monkey cautiously stands at the edge of the soft muck and slides the rope-like plant to her. Grabbing hold, Alexa breathes a sigh of relief, as she attempts to pull herself out of the mud.

The vine pulls tight, briefly lifting her up, but then loosens and slacks. She grips, hand over hand, pulling more and more vegetation from the jungle while sinking deeper. Curtiss puts his hands on his head and begins to jump up and down, screeching as he watches her drop lower. Alexa takes a deep breath, as the watery muck creeps just below the bottom of her chin.

Chapter 24

An hour before sunset, golden rays of light shimmer above the ocean horizon, across the calm, southern seas. The pirate Catalina seaplane, dark and quiet, idly floats a bit further off-shore, just past Quint's sailing sloop. Both vessels cast long, distinct shadows on the seaweed-choked waters that hug the island coastline.

At the entry to the cockpit, inside the seaplane, Merrill stands next to the communications radio, holding a pair of headphones to his ear. A satisfied grin melts his stone-cold features, as he watches the radio operator lean into the microphone to respond, "Copy that, A. P. Two-Twenty, out."

The static on the radio fades out as Merrill drops the earpieces, letting them dangle from the connecting cord. With an ominous chuckle, he turns away.

~*~

A vine connected to a cluster of trees creaks with strain. Alexa holds tight, while trying to keep her mouth clear of the muddy sludge. With her head tilted back and the swampy surface rising above her ears, Alexa's only view is that of the colorful evening sky through the clearing above.

Alexa notices the thumping sensation of the elevated pulse pounding in her chest, and begins to feel some panic. Her pressed lips hover just over the surface. Tears of lament flood her eyes, as they roll over to the sight of the air pirate's hand dangling in the air.

"What a terrible way for me to die..."

Alexa feels a steady tug on the vine, and she clings tighter to it as she is slowly pulled higher. "Is that you, Curtiss?" As her face clears the surface, Alexa tilts her mud-covered chin to see Jimmy standing at the side of the pit, grinning as he tugs on her lifeline.

"Miss me much?"

Desperately gripping the vine, Alexa cries with happiness at the sight of her seaplane pilot. She trembles with emotion, as he pulls her free from the life-sucking mud and brings her in close to him. "Hey there..."

Face-to-face, the two hold each other tightly and Jimmy wipes the sludge from under Alexa's muddy chin. They gaze passionately into each other's eyes for a moment, until Alexa breaks from the trance and wipes a lock of mud-covered hair from her temple. She attempts to hide her flood of emotions and pushes away from him. "I thought you were dead."

"Not yet."

Alexa quickly composes herself and wriggles from Jimmy's embrace. "Thank you, Captain Ferral."

A tug at the leg of her pants diverts her attention, and Curtiss wraps his arms around her knee. She looks down and takes the monkey's hand. There is a brief glance at Jimmy before she turns and walks toward the trampled jungle path.

Jimmy looks over at the swampy pit, grabs the machine gun from the surface of the mud pit, and nonchalantly salutes the outstretched pirate appendage. He watches Alexa walk away, as he gives a sigh of acceptance. "Sure, no problem."

~*~

Sunset brings somewhat tolerable temperatures and lower humidity to the island. Jimmy and Alexa hike through the thick jungle brush, their clothing heavy with wet patches of sweat and drying mud. Jimmy keeps his pistol tucked in his belt while carrying the pirate's automatic rifle.

Alexa follows with Curtiss clinging to her shoulders like a backpack. As they near the end of the trail, Jimmy pauses to listen. Alexa moves up behind him and speaks in a cautious tone. "Are we close to where we left the boat?"

"I think so. The underbrush seems to thin out ahead. We need to stay off the cut path, so we don't run into anymore of those pirate crewmen."

Alexa scans her surroundings before urging Curtiss to climb down from her back. She leans over to speak with Jimmy. "Do you think the boat is still there?"

He glances back at her with a worried expression. "Hate to say it, but I hope not."

~*~

The sun sits at the horizon as Jimmy and Alexa creep up to the coastline to get a better vantage of the open water. The tethered sailboat sits calmly afloat on the high tide, several yards out from the shore. They identify a single pirate on the deck guarding a crumpled body lashed to an overturned chair. The Catalina seaplane is anchored nearby.

Alexa whispers to Jimmy, "Is that Quint?"

"Yeah." He shakes his head and looks down to squash a spider with the butt of the machine gun.

Feeling responsible for Quint's situation, Alexa keeps a sensitive tone. "What do you think?"

Jimmy clenches his jaw and turns to her, his eyes flashing hot with a burning intensity. "We're going to grab Quint and get the hell out of here."

"Do you have a plan?" Alexa watches as Jimmy removes the backpack and tucks his pistol inside.

"It's a work in progress." He takes the machine gun, quietly cocks it, and hands it to Alexa. "Whatever you see or hear, don't come near that boat unless I wave you over." Jimmy slowly slides down the rocky shoreline and into the waist-deep water. "Stay here. I'll be right back."

Alexa studies the automatic rifle and then looks toward the water vessels. As the algae-covered water laps gently against the shore, she watches Jimmy slide his arms back through the shoulder straps of the bag before asking, "Do you want to leave the pack here?"

"I better hold on to it."

"Wouldn't it be easier to swim without it?"

"Just stay put. Use that if you have to."

Jimmy nods toward the machine gun and then eases farther into the seaweed-thick water. He plunges quietly in, just under the surface toward Quint's sailboat.

~*~

From the shelter of the coastline vegetation, Alexa patiently watches as Jimmy swims, undetected, up to the sailboat hull. She looks back at Curtiss, who is studying a nearby spider. She gets his attention and quietly warns him. "Curtiss, leave that thing alone. They're dangerous."

The monkey grins at her and leaves his hand poised over the flowery arachnid. He finds the spider quite entertaining. The creature seems to return the look of amusement, then turns and scurries away.

Jimmy uses the boat as a visual barrier between himself and the seaplane. He swims quietly and eases around the hull to a location that lines-up with Quint's slumped body. At the surface of the water, near the bow, Jimmy grabs hold of the anchor tether and pulls himself up to the railing. He peeks over the deck and sees the pirate guard sitting atop the cabin, facing the stern, enjoying the last hint of color fade along the horizon.

After noiselessly slipping over the rail, Jimmy, dripping wet, crawls slowly toward Quint and begins to cut him loose. He leans down low and whispers, almost inaudibly, "Quint, can you hear me?"

Jimmy cuts through the ties on his wrists, and Quint slumps free from the chair. As Jimmy wipes the long hair back from Quint's face, a blood-crusted eye opens slightly. "Jimmy... Where the hell you been?"

"We're getting out of here. You stay put a minute until I get us going."

Quint silently nods, nary moving a muscle.

Moving stealthily, Jimmy works his way along the deck of the gently rolling sailboat. He slips behind the cabin and peeks to see the pirate reclined, enjoying the evening breeze. Slowly, he creeps up onto the cabin and sneaks toward the unsuspecting pirate.

Suddenly, the air pirate opens his eyes and the two men exchange expressions of surprise. Jimmy lunges and slams his fist into the pirate's jaw, smashing the man's head to the roof of the cabin. Reaching back for another blow, Jimmy pauses as he realizes that the man is unconscious.

~*~

From the bushes along the shoreline, Alexa watches as Jimmy drags the limp pirate down into the boat's cabin. Movement near the floating seaplane catches her attention. She sees Merrill and two pirates climb into the inflatable raft. With Merrill positioned in the middle, holding a handgun across his lap, the pirate crewmen paddle in the direction of Quint's sailboat. Merrill cocks the firearm and conceals it in the holster under his jacket.

With no way to warn Jimmy, Alexa waits anxiously, watching for signs of movement on the boat. There is a rustle in the bushes behind her, and Alexa turns to see Curtiss disappear into the jungle. In a low voice, Alexa hisses, "Curtiss... Curtiss, where are you going?", and receives no response.

Alexa turns to watch as the inflatable raft rows closer to the sailboat. She shakes her head and looks down at the automatic rifle. A look of heroic determination crosses her features, as she quietly moves into the water while slinging the heavy machine gun onto her shoulder. "C'mon, Jimmy... Do something... They're coming." Alexa slips into the pale, seaweed-filled waters and quietly swims with a layer of encrusted mud washing away.

Chapter 25

The dinghy thuds against the sailboat. Merrill climbs aboard the boat, followed by his henchmen. They all stand at the helm, searching the ship's deck for the pirate who was left on guard. Merrill's eyes squint skeptically at the thought of someone disobeying his orders. His eyes scan the deck, and he notices a strange lump with a tail on the silhouetted shadow of the main mast.

Merrill's gaze rises up to the furry figure of Curtiss clinging at the top of the mainsail. The pirate looks to shore and determines the jump from the nearest tree on the coastline would have been an incredible leap of faith. In a quiet standoff, Merrill and Curtiss stare at each other until the first mate opens his jacket and removes the cocked pistol from his shoulder rig. His eyes lower back to the ship's deck, and then he looks over the side rail to the water below.

Merrill's gaze travels to Quint, still sprawled out in the chair near the front of the cabin. Without turning to the pirate crew behind him, he growls in a low voice. "I thought I told that man to keep a watch."

The two pirates stand, looking around for their missing shipmate, while Merrill moves toward the sailboat's bow, where Quint still lies on the deck.

Merrill murmurs to himself, as he strides across the vessel. "No matter... He won't require watching any longer." He stands over Quint, staring down at him momentarily before calling to the men waiting at the stern, "Get him up."

Quint holds the severed ropes around his wrists, as one of the men pulls him and the chair upright. The pirate first mate moves forward and slaps Quint hard across the face. His head jerked to the side, Quint slowly opens his eyes as he cracks a blood-covered smile.

A hint of surprise flickers across Merrill's face, and he raises the pistol to his waist. He aims the gun barrel at Quint's head as their eyes meet. "I don't know why you are smiling. Captain Rasmus says he has no use for you whatsoever."

When Merrill's finger begins to tense on the trigger, Quint quickly swings out, knocking the pistol from his hand. The gun fires as it hits the deck, and the stray bullet splinters one of the wooden rails. Merrill and the two pirates stand, dumbfounded, as the gun skitters several feet across the deck.

Quint stands and swings his fist out, hitting Merrill square in the chin, knocking him backward against the mast. The pirates raise their machine guns and Jimmy pops up from the other side of the ship's cabin. Aiming his gun, he yells, "Hold it!"

The pirates turn their automatic weapons toward the cabin, as Quint rubs his clenched fist tenderly. He glances over at Jimmy. "Where the hell have you been?"

"What do you mean?"

Quint stands before Merrill, who stares at him through malevolent eyes.

"I mean... What the hell?"

One of the air pirates steals a glance toward Merrill, who nods. As Quint reaches for Merrill's gun on the deck, the pirates suddenly open fire toward the sailboat's main cabin. Jimmy snaps off two shots, hitting one of the machine gunners in the thigh before ducking down for cover behind the cabin. While a hail of bullets tear into the ship's living quarters, Quint delivers a raised knee to Merrill's gut before leaping, unarmed, over the side-rail.

Merrill recovers his breath and grabs his loose pistol. He glances over the side to the vacant water below and then, in a smoky haze of burnt gunpowder, turns to the bullet-riddled cabin. He puts up his hand and gestures for the pirates to cease their shooting. "Hold your fire!"

The two pirates lower their smoking-hot gun barrels and move closer to the wreckage at the center of the sailboat. The unwounded pirate moves around to the hatch and looks down into the darkness below. The other pirate limps after Merrill as he scans the empty waters surrounding the sailboat. The air pirate at the cabin hatch smiles and waves to them both. "Looks like we got him."

Merrill steps around to the hatch and stares down into the interior, speckled with dim lighting from the bullet holes. He turns and grabs the pirate by the neck. "Was he bound and gagged when he shot at you?"

"No…"

"Then it's not him, is it?"

While one pirate is being throttled, the other holds his injured leg, backs away, and looks over the stern of the boat. A single gunshot rings out, and the pirate reels back as a forty-five auto slug pierces through his forehead.

Merrill and the remaining pirate drop to the deck and look at their dead crewmate sprawled out on the boards. Pistol in hand, Merrill motions to the back of the sailboat. "He's over the side!" They creep to the edge of the ship deck and peek over to see Jimmy and Quint in the rubber dinghy. The men onboard duck back, as several shots rip past them, splintering the aft railing.

Rolling clear, Merrill waves a command and the pirate points his machine gun over the side and empties it blindly. Ears still ringing from the blast, Merrill calls to the punctured raft below. "Give it up. You can't win."

After a brief pause, Jimmy responds to the pirate, "Depends what you mean by winning."

Jimmy and Quint tuck themselves close to the hull of the sailboat, as the rubber dinghy slowly deflates. Jimmy swings the backpack around to the front and digs out another clip of ammunition. He tucks it in his shirt pocket and looks up at the railing, ready to take another potshot at the pirates. Jimmy aims his gun high and yells up to the sailboat deck. "What do you want?"

There is a looming silence on the boat, as the air pirate reloads a straight-stick ammo clip into the auto machine gun. Staring ahead as he calmly reloads his pistol, Merrill pulls back the bolt on the gun, and hollers over the side to Jimmy. "Rasmus will be here soon. He just wants the girl."

"She's still on the island."

"We'll find her."

"She's dead."

Jimmy glances at his wet and bloody friend, winking and shaking his head when Quint gapes at him inquiringly. Gun raised high, Jimmy watches the upper deck railing and calls out, "You can just let us go now. The prize is gone."

Gun cocked and loaded, Merrill looks to the pirate next to him. Touching his bruised jaw and grimacing, he responds. "No, Captain. Now you have nothing to bargain with."

As Merrill and the air pirate stand with their guns, ready to shoot over the rail, large caliber machine gunfire fills the air with a series of deafening blasts. Before they can discharge their weapons, the two pirates are riddled with bullets while the wood decking around them splinters and shreds in a hail of debris.

Jimmy and Quint hunker down low under the flashing tracers and then turn to the pirate seaplane. The dual thirty caliber guns at the nose turret are still hot and smoking, as Alexa pokes her head out of the front hatch. After looking around for any surviving targets, she smiles at the men in the half-deflated rubber dinghy. "Bet you boys are glad to see me."

Quint gawks at the bullet-shattered decking of his wrecked sailboat and back to Alexa, grinning, seemingly quite pleased with herself. Her dripping-wet clothes cling to her as she hoists herself out of the nose turret, leans back on the Catalina's foredeck, and pulls her feet out of the hatch. "Sometimes it takes a woman to get the job done right."

Exasperated, Quint slams his fist on the hull of his sailboat. "You just shot the hell out of my boat!"

Alexa stands and looks across at the sailboat wreckage. She waves to the furry copilot at the top of the sail rigging and then down to the men comically standing in the half-sunk inflatable raft. "It's just a boat, Quint. I'll get you another."

The battered mariner silently fumes as he studies the gaping cavity ripped into the hull of his boat by the seaplane's high caliber machine guns. Jimmy takes a deep breath and looks down at the water rushing in as the raft steadily sinks. "Yeah, Quint... It's just a boat."

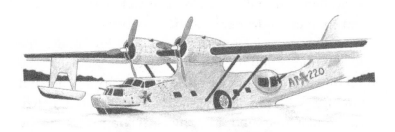

Chapter 26

Inside the pirate Catalina seaplane, several glowing lights illuminate the cockpit. Jimmy slides in behind the controls and looks over the panel slowly. Curtiss crawls into the copilot chair and readies for flight by scratching at the seat cushion to make it more comfortable. Entering from behind the captain's chairs, Quint and Alexa look over Jimmy's shoulder. She leans down and, in a low voice, whispers, "Can you fly this thing?"

Quint stifles a laugh and moves back to the radio controller's seat. He rests his battered head against the bulkhead and stares through the window fondly at his destroyed sailboat. Jimmy winks over his shoulder at Quint, and they exchange a knowing glance. "I just need to take a minute to adjust."

Jimmy whistles quietly, as he runs his hand over several controls, changes a few knob settings, and sits back again to study the panel. Watching impatiently, Alexa looks outside to the hint of twinkling stars and then back to Jimmy. "If Captain Rasmus is indeed on his way, don't you think you should adjust a little faster and get us out of here?"

He glances up at her hovering over his shoulder and shakes his head, annoyed. "Quit breathing down my neck." The pilot turns and gives a commanding tilt of his head to Quint, who smiles in return. With a grunt, the aching sailor stands, gives Jimmy a half-hearted salute, and makes his exit to the cargo hold of the seaplane. Jimmy continues fiddling with the illuminated controls and starts his preflight check. "This isn't like driving a damn city bus or something. Why don't you visit with Quint in the back? Make yourself useful and help him get cleaned up."

Feeling awkward, she stands behind Jimmy and then looks down at Curtiss, firmly occupying the copilot's chair. "Are you sure you don't need my help?"

"Positive."

Jimmy grabs a headset, snaps it over his ears, and resumes his preflight check. The furry copilot dons another pair of earphones, mimicking Jimmy. She watches awhile, and then gives Curtiss a friendly pat before exiting the cockpit. "All right, then. I'll leave you two at it."

~*~

The cargo-hold of the seaplane is set up like a barracks. Attached on the curved walls are folding bunks which hang from the bulkhead, racks of guns, and cases of ammunition. The midsection of the seaplane has blister windows on the port and starboard sides and stations for a waist gunner to maneuver the protruding large-caliber machine guns.

Quint sits at the post of the ship's first mate, a small operations desk illuminated by a bulkhead lamp. He sorts through an open medical kit, searching for bandages and stitching supplies. Under the work-light, Quint peers down at the small mirror in the lid of the kit and winces, as he wipes his blood-encrusted eye. Alexa walks over and sits on one of the nearby bunks.

"I am sorry about your boat."

He holds a compress to the cut over his eye and nods. "I can sell this warbird and get a new one."

Alexa smiles and leans in to inspect Quint's wound. "Need some help with that?"

"Considering that both my eyes are beat to hell and 'bout swollen shut, yes."

Alexa slides from her seat and kneels alongside Quint. She takes a swab from him and angles the light on the wall. Not sure where to start, she begins by cleaning his worst eye. He flinches at her touch and she grimaces as she clears his skin of the dried blood, reopening the recent wound. "You might need some stitches."

"I didn't see a needle and thread in there. You'll just have to tape it best you can."

She pours a spot of water from a metal canteen onto the cloth and wipes the dark crust from his face. While cleaning the battered sea-dog, she looks ahead to the cockpit and curiously asks, "How long have you known Jimmy?"

"Since the war."

"You two fly together?"

Quint pulls back from her touch and appears offended. "Do I look like a flyboy?"

She shrugs, continuing to dab gently at his injured face. "What did you do during the war?"

"I was at the base he flew out from. I *acquired* things." He gives her a sly smile.

Alexa looks quizzical. "For who?"

"Whoever was in need and paying the most at the time. Mostly the government or private companies."

Quint winces, as Alexa applies some stitch-strip bandages over one of his gaping cuts. He smiles affably, while he fondly reminisces on his wartime career. "Was pretty good at it, too. I found that plane of Jimmy's."

"The seaplane?"

"Yep. He'd probably be living a normal life stateside and have about six kids by now, if that Grumman amphibian hadn't come along."

Alexa giggles, amused. "Think so?"

"Oh, yeah. He loves that airplane." A metal flask appears from the desk cubby and Quint gives it a tilted shake before opening the lid. He takes a cautious sniff and chances a swig, blinking his swollen eyes as the burn of island-brewed liquor gives him a shiver. Quint pulls back and lets the heat settle in, as Alexa tries to apply another adhesive bandage. She waits, with the dressing held ready, while he wriggles his face under the medical tape. Quint gives her a knowing look and smiles. "He must like you an awful lot to get that bird shot up and then leave it on my island, unattended."

Alexa looks slightly embarrassed, and she casts her eyes away. The dark shadows of the cargo-hold play across her face, as she continues applying clean bandages across Quint's cheek. "Probably just really needed the money."

He notices her blushing some and tilts his head playfully. "I doubt it. He does all right. Cargo jobs are fairly easy to come by around here since the war. Hell, the way he lives... Well, the money lasts quite a while."

"Yes, his place was an interesting wreck."

"His home is at the controls of that seaplane."

"I guess that is kind of exciting."

"Sometimes."

"Do you think he'll ever change?"

The body of the PBY Catalina seaplane begins to tremble as the engines fire up and the propellers start to spin. Quint looks at Alexa in the shadowy light of the cargo hold. "You never know when one life ends and another begins."

The thunder of both engines roaring, the black-painted pirate Catalina seaplane moves slowly across moonlit waters. The dark, silhouette of the high-winged aircraft leaves the uncharted island and ruined, half-sunken sailboat in its watery wake as it picks up speed. Once out to open seas, it step-taxies for a stretch, and, with ocean spray peeling off its hull, lifts into the star-filled sky.

Chapter 27

The brilliant orange orb of the sun begins to emerge on the horizon in the eastern sky. Jimmy sits behind the controls of the commandeered pirate seaplane, as it flies over the water through the early light of day. The morning brightness causes his eyes to squint, as he looks over at Curtiss, sleeping in the copilot seat with headphones still clamped over his ears.

The sun beams in brightly as Alexa enters the cockpit. She quietly stands behind Jimmy and puts her hand on the back of his chair. Her other hand shades her eyes from the sun, and she looks out the forward windows. She points to a dark spot emerging from the wispy clouds on the horizon. "What's that?"

Jimmy wipes the drowsiness from his face and focuses his gaze on the small object in the distance. All is quiet but for the drone of the plane's overhead engines. Quint enters from the back to sit by the radio, as Jimmy shakes his head and rubs his eyes again. "Damn..."

Curtiss rouses and wakes as Alexa leans over his chair. She scrunches her face, as she studies the tiny speck in the distant sky. "Looks like an airplane."

Quint moves up and looks out the window. He grunts, as he touches the tender bandages on his face. "That's an aircraft, all right. Rasmus, ya think?"

Shocked, Alexa looks at Quint. "Is that possible?"

"Anything's possible…"

"Maybe they haven't seen us." As the words leave her lips, the radio begins to light up, crackle, and come to life. Everyone turns to look as the electronics begin to hum with a weak transmission. "A. P. Two-Twenty, do you copy?"

Static follows, as they all stare in silence. A frightening realization occurs to them before the radio crackles again. "Come in A. P. Catalina Two-Twenty, this is Catalina P. M. R., Do you copy?"

Alexa turns to Jimmy, horrified. "You flew us right to them! What is wrong with you?!?"

"What do you mean, *wrong with me*?"

"How are you going to get us out of this now?"

Flabbergasted, Jimmy looks up at Alexa, and turns to Quint by the radio. His mind reels, as Quint sits down and picks up the handheld receiver. He blurts out. "Don't answer it!"

Quint nods, as Curtiss tosses off his headphones and jumps from the copilot chair. The monkey stands, half-awake. Then, alarmed by the voice from the radio, he scampers past them to the rear cargo area. Infuriated, Alexa takes Curtiss's seat and stares at Jimmy. "Pretend we're not home? Is that your mastermind of a plan?!? They've obviously seen us!"

Jimmy rips off his headset and turns to Alexa with a hard, scolding glare. Then, he swivels around in his seat. Seeing that Quint is still watching the radio set light up and crackle with life, Jimmy suggests, "Click the receiver a few times and give 'em some static."

The receiver hums with empty static. Quint clicks a few more times before looking back to Jimmy for instructions. Alexa appears like she is ready to burst with rage, as she sits watching them. Quint shushes her with a finger to his lips, nodding as he puts the receiver down. Indignant, Alexa leans over in the copilot chair to taunt Jimmy. "After flying all night, you flew us right into their lap?"

Jimmy shakes his head and growls, "How the hell was I supposed to know where they were?"

With his face bandaged all over and taped together, Quint relaxes into the radio operator chair, staying clear of Jimmy and Alexa, in front, who seem to want the chance at throwing the other out of the plane.

Barely able to contain herself, Alexa grips the armrest of the copilot chair and makes an attempt to speak calmly. "Can we outrun them?"

"Who knows how much fuel they might have aboard? We barely have enough to make it anywhere remotely close."

Quint raises his hand and yells to them. "If we're headed to a refueling location, they've probably come from that very spot and have full tanks."

Alexa sarcastically smiles at Quint before turning to scowl at Jimmy. "Our situation keeps getting better."

Jimmy looks back at Quint and rolls his eyes at him. "Thank you, Quint. That was, *oh so very helpful.*"

Breathing through clenched teeth, Alexa glares at Jimmy before turning her gaze toward the approaching seaplane. "So, first you lose the headpiece, we barely escape with our lives, and then you lead us right back to the psychotic air pirates who are trying to kill us?"

Jimmy's eyes flare with resentment. "Hey now, that's not fair!"

"Which part isn't true?"

Jimmy slams his fist on the console. He rechecks the instruments, as Alexa, sits back and crosses her arms.

The engines rumble and everyone stares ahead, as the aircraft in the distance gets closer. Alexa turns to Jimmy and smiles insincerely. "So Captain, what's your plan now?"

"We'll ease up, save fuel, and let them come and catch us."

"That's your great idea?"

Jimmy turns to look at Quint, who shrugs indifferently. Jimmy points a finger to the cargo area and gestures to his friend. "Check out those fifty-caliber guns and see what kind of ammo we have aboard."

"Aye aye, Captain."

Quint eases out of the radio controller's chair and moves back through the aircraft to the starboard gun position. Alexa turns to Jimmy. "Are you crazy?"

His hand reaches overhead to pull back the throttles. Ignoring Alexa, he concentrates on syncing the engines and reserving fuel.

"No."

"You realize these pirates make their living by shooting people out of the sky..."

"It's harder than you think... Besides, they don't know who's in here. By the time they realize it's us, we'll have given them something to think about."

"So, just wait and hopefully surprise them?"

"We won't go wagging our gun barrels to tip 'em off." Jimmy looks to Alexa and can't help but admire her attempt at composure during their time of distress. Hey, why don't you move back there and help Quint?"

"You don't want my company?"

He smiles at her wryly. "Send Curtiss up!"

~*~

The two Catalina seaplanes circle around and catch up to each other. Jimmy sits at the controls with Curtiss seated next to him in the copilot chair. Turning to the cargo area, he hollers over the din of engine noise, "How's it going back there?"

Quint leans out from the starboard gunner position and gives a thumbs-up. "Locked and loaded! How soon?"

"They're almost on us!"

"Just give me the word!"

Jimmy waves and turns forward. "Copy that!"

Seated at the radio controller's station, Alexa watches as the panel lights up and crackles again. "A. P. Two-Twenty, this is Catalina P. M. R. Can you read us?"

Just before the pirate seaplane comes alongside, Jimmy shouts over his shoulder to Alexa, "Give them a few clicks!"

She gives the receiver several clicks and sets it down again as the radio transmitter crackles, "A. P. Two-Twenty, we're approaching on your starboard side to give visual instructions. Over."

Staring back through one of the portal windows, Jimmy waits as the pirate aircraft moves closer. "Better strap yourself in, honey! It's going to get a little bumpy!"

Biting his lip, he pulls his seat harness tighter. Jimmy grips the control yoke, looks behind and hollers over his shoulder to the cargo hold. "Ready, Quint?"

At the starboard blister turret, Quint steadies his hands on the gunnery grips, careful not to move the barrel and give away the surprise. He yells forward, "You betcha!"

Jimmy leans over to look at Quint standing ready at the gunner position. "Wait for my signal!"

"Copy that, Captain."

Engines rumbling, Jimmy pushes back in his chair seat. He glances out the side window, next to Curtiss, as the pirate Catalina slowly eases up alongside.

Alexa leans forward to whisper loudly, "You're a good pilot, Jimmy. I know you'll get us out of here."

Jimmy smiles nervously. "Yeah, sure…"

Chapter 28

The twin radial engines roar, as the two large seaplanes fly alongside one another, sending a tingle of wartime adrenaline through Jimmy's body. The two warplanes fly in formation, closer and closer, until their wingtips almost touch. Thundering through the sky, the two black Catalina PBY flying-boats soar over the calm, blue ocean.

Through the starboard window, Jimmy catches the confused expressions of the air pirates piloting the other plane. Standing on his seat, Curtiss presses his face to the window and shows his teeth. Jimmy waves a dismissive salute to the stunned pilots and calls back to the cargo area. "All right, Quint! Let 'em have it!"

The air pirates' confusion morphs into horror as Quint unloads the machine gun toward the enemy's mid-section. Bullets tear into wings and fuselage, as the pirate seaplane immediately banks and drops away. Alexa stands to watch them through the window.

"They're running away!"

Quint continues to fire on the pirates, until the flaming tracers from the fifty caliber machine gun drop short of the fleeing target.

Jimmy, looking somewhat relieved, turns to Alexa. "They're chased off, but they'll be back."

"We gave them a taste of their own medicine."

Jimmy smiles at her and then, over his shoulder, yells, "Quint! Great job! Load 'er up again!" Dipping the starboard wing, Jimmy peers out the window, as the pirate Catalina flies away into the distance.

~*~

A clatter of ammunition belts echoes off the metal walls of the seaplane, as Quint readies the side-turret gun for another encounter. He feeds the long string of five-inch cartridges into the breech and glances over, as Alexa moves back into the cargo hold. The bandaged sailor at the gun port beams at her, and pulls back the bolt, arming the weapon. "Now, that was fun. Wasn't able to give 'em the whole nine yards, but I doubt they're seaworthy anymore."

"Need any help back here?"

Quint steps aside from the midsection gunner position and gestures for her to take the controls.

"Yeah… Take over this gun."

"What?"

He ushers her nearer to the gun, and she puts her hands to the metal grips. Quint stands close behind her, talking over her shoulder. "They're going to be coming back around soon. I have to get the other guns ready. When they fly near enough, use it." He puts his arms around her and helps to move the gun up, down and around. Quint's breath tickles her neck and sends gooseflesh up her arm. "All you have to do is line them up here and squeeze."

Alexa looks down the sights. "Simple enough."

"You'd think so. It's like throwing spitballs in the wind. Don't waste the shots if they're too far away."

Enclosed in his arms, she looks over her shoulder. "How will I know if they're close enough?"

Quint steps back from his embrace, and gives a wink. "They'll be shooting at us." He taps his fingers on the metal receiver and moves toward the gun setup in the nose turret.

~*~

In the cockpit, Jimmy nervously watches for the return of the pirate Catalina. He looks over to see Curtiss frozen in the copilot seat and Jimmy flashes a paternal smile, in an attempt to reduce the anxiety of his furry friend. Glancing over his shoulder to the rear hold, he sees Alexa standing at the waist-gunner position.

Her hands are clamped onto the cold, metal gun grips, as she stares out into the empty, blue firmament. She looks behind to the portside gun-blister and does a double take. "Guys... There they are!" Jimmy anxiously scans out the forward and side windows before hollering back to her. "Where? I don't see 'em!"

She points to one of the portside windows and jabs her finger toward the approaching pirate seaplane "Right there!"

"Dammit! What's the position to us? What time?"

Alexa looks confused as she shouts up to the cockpit. "When?!? Very soon!!!"

Alexa stands, shocked, as Jimmy dashes from the front and looks to where she points. He chops his hand in the air, representing a flat clock face. "Twelve o'clock, nine o'clock, seven o'clock! They're at seven o'clock!!!" Alexa stares in blank confusion, and Jimmy, frustrated, shakes his head. "Never mind."

Alexa peeks down the corridor toward Quint, still at the nose, and then at Jimmy. "Who's flying?"

"Curtiss…"

"Get back up there, Captain!"

Jimmy runs back to the cockpit, and Alexa moves over and positions herself behind the portside machine gun blister. As Quint had earlier demonstrated, she heaves the bolt back and lets it slam forward into the armed position. With the pirate seaplane lined-up in her sights, she waits nervously as it slowly approaches.

Returned to the cockpit, Jimmy slides into the captain chair and looks over to see Curtiss' small hands on the yoke and steering the airplane. He straps himself in, offers an appreciative nod, and takes over the wheel. He looks past his left shoulder and out the rear portside window, apprehensively watching as the air pirates steadily approach. "Quint, how's it going down there? They're coming up on us again!"

Quint's muted voice hails from the nose turret position. "This double-thirty is all jammed up! It's going to take another minute to clear it!"

Alexa leans back from her gunner position and shouts. "We don't *have* another minute! They're *right there*!!!"

Through the portside window, Jimmy watches as the other seaplane gets dangerously close. The pirates fire, and several shots puncture the metal skin of the stolen airplane. "Aw, dammit... I'm getting really tired of being shot at!" Jimmy pushes the steering yoke forward and dives the aircraft, gaining speed and distance. As the fleeing seaplane banks away, a bullet grazes the windshield, cracking it.

Jimmy yells to the gunner position. "Fire, Alexa! Fire!!!"

Alexa braces herself and maneuvers her gun to target the pursuing seaplane. She squeezes the trigger and releases a burst of gunfire. A surge of euphoria sweeps through her, as the projectiles find their mark. "Jimmy, I think I got them!"

Jimmy looks back over his shoulder and gestures a thumbs up. "Good job! Keep firing!"

As Alexa continues to fire the large machine gun, the pirate seaplane returns fire from its starboard waist-gun and the dual thirty-caliber nose gun turret. Flaming tracers from each of the guns zip through the air between the airplanes. Both aircrafts take several superficial hits.

From the port window, Jimmy can see tracer rounds flashing between the two seaplanes. He adjusts the duel-engine throttles and tries to outmaneuver his attackers. Pushing his feet on the elevator control pedals as if he's climbing stairs, Jimmy yells to the nose section. "Quint! What the hell are you doing down there?"

"I'm workin', dammit!"

After several metallic clangs and a lot of cursing, Quint pops his head into the cockpit. He shakes his head, swipes his hair back from his face, and slaps the back of Jimmy's chair. "Better keep runnin'… The nose gun's busted all to hell."

Quint looks back to Alexa handling the fifty-caliber machine gun and smiles. "*She's* doin' all right…"

As Jimmy maneuvers the controls, the seaplane bobs in the sky, becoming a more difficult target. He glances back to Alexa and asks, "Does she know what the hell she's doing?"

"Do any of us?"

"Get back there!"

"Aye, aye Captain." Chuckling, Quint ducks out of the cockpit and back into the cargo hold.

The two Catalina seaplanes dip and weave through the air, trying to disable the other. Tracers fly in every direction, and several hit their intended mark. The strained engines roar, as Jimmy dives and banks. The plinking sound of hot lead is heard, and daylight streams through holes in the haze-filled fuselage. Behind the side blister turret, Alexa continues to fire the machine gun, her arms and body tiring from the effort.

After being knocked from his feet several times, Quint grabs the overhead rails to brace himself. Alexa leans back in the gunner harness and gestures to the empty machine gun. Quint deftly reloads the hot gun and turns it back to Alexa. She slams back the bolt, as an explosion suddenly rocks the seaplane in the air. The left engine bursts with flames and an ominous stream of dark smoke trails behind.

In the cockpit, Curtiss jumps up and down in his seat, covering his eyes as Jimmy cuts the fuel supply to the engine. As the propeller limply spins in the breeze, thick clouds of black smoke blow back from the hot, flaming engine cowl. Quint steps into the cockpit, grabbing hold of the radio table for balance. He looks up, through the overhead windows, to the burning radial. "We lose that engine?"

"Yeah, we're not going to last long up here..."

"That's good."

Jimmy looks over his shoulder questioningly. "Why?"

"We don't have much big ammo left either."

"Aww, hell..."

Quint shrugs his shoulders and touches the patchwork of bandages on his face. "They stocked this raft more for intimidation on the high seas than for battle." He leans forward and points to a piece of land on the watery horizon. "Bring us in there."

"I don't know if we can make it that far."

The sailor reaches over to give the furry copilot a quick rub on the belly, laughs nervously, and pats Jimmy on the shoulder. "Sure we can, Jimmy... You're a heck of a good pilot."

As the stalwart sailor exits the cockpit, Jimmy gives him a sidelong glance. "I wish I had your amount of faith..."

Chapter 29

The two bullet-riddled seaplanes continue to battle in close formation, while flying toward the island on the horizon. The pirate Catalina keeps up its lethal machine gun fire and the stolen seaplane flees, powered by a single engine. Trailing slightly to the rear, the air pirates continue the assault, using alternate attacking angles while firing the nose-turret and waist side-blister guns.

Quint loads the starboard gun, braces himself on the harness, and clicks off a burst of gunfire. To avoid the volley, the pirates dive away, loop under and around to return on the other side. Alexa lets go several rounds of fire with the port-side gun until it clicks empty.

"I need another set of rounds!"

The bandaged sailor tosses hollow ammunition boxes aside and grabs up the last belt of cartridges. He slams the strip of ammunition into the gun and hands off the loaded weapon to Alexa. "This is the last one…"

"What? Really?"

Quint pats her on the shoulder and returns to his spot at the port-side gun-turret. "That's okay. We're about to crash anyway."

Alexa peers over her shoulder at Quint, trying to make out if he's jesting. He shrugs apathetically and rips off a deafening blast from the automatic gun. The attacking pirates dodge the gunfire and dip low under the leading aircraft's tail. Alexa gets a brief glimpse of the attacking seaplane and squeezes the trigger. The target falls away, out of range, and continues its pursuit.

Quint leans outward to keep eyes on their attackers and yells behind to Alexa. "Darlin', you better run up front and strap yerself in!"

Several bullets whiz through the floor of the cargo area, sending metal canisters and debris flying. A piece of shrapnel catches Quint in the leg, and Alexa rushes to him as he crumples over in pain. She inspects the bloody gash on his thigh until Quint dismissively pushes her aside and moves back to his defensive position at the waist gun. He hollers over the sputtering rumble of the seaplane's remaining engine. "Time for you to move up front, Missy!"

"But you're injured…"

"I'm fine. I'll finish up back here. Go on!"

Alexa watches a moment, as he puts out a heavy stream of gunfire on the pirates. The attacking pirate warplane dives under the tracers and comes up again on the opposing side. Hobbling across to the port-side gun, Quint waves Alexa away and covers their flank with a blast from the blister gun. "Git up there. I got this!"

~*~

Several rounds of hot lead whiz through the fuselage, as Alexa runs into the cockpit. She stands behind the captain's chair and looks through the upper panel of windows at the smoking engine and idly spiraling, bullet-damaged prop. Jimmy reaches to adjust the throttle of the remaining engine, as Alexa looks ahead toward the small island in the near distance. Her voice calls out over the roar of the single radial engine, "Are we going to crash?"

Jimmy looks up from the controls and shakes his head. "Naw, we're going in for a rough ... very rough, rough landing."

Alexa scoots Curtiss from the copilot's chair and straps herself in tightly. Jimmy dives the yoke of the seaplane, dropping it to mere feet above the ocean waves. With growing panic, Alexa watches as they quickly approach the landmass. "We're going to crash into that island!"

Concentrating on flying the airplane, Jimmy retorts, "Okay..."

The island looms steadily closer, as the two seaplanes race just above the surface of the rolling, aqua-blue waters. The pirate seaplane continues to unleash lethal spurts of gunfire while trailing just off the rear flank. Zigzagging in tight formation, the two aircrafts dive lower and skim the tips of the swelling waves.

With a grunt, Quint stumbles through the oval doorway of the cockpit and takes a seat at the radio controller's station. He fumbles with the seat harness buckle, as he hollers forward to Jimmy and Alexa.

"That's it for that. We've unloaded all the big guns aboard this ship."

Jimmy looks behind at him and sees the bloodied leg. "You hit?"

"As long as you don't put us in the drink where there is a pattern of shark fins, I'll be fine." Quint finishes strapping himself in and pulls Curtiss to his lap.

The two seaplanes approach the island, and Jimmy dips the Catalina into the ocean waves. The pirate seaplane follows closely, briefly ceasing fire. Jimmy bounces the flying boat across the ocean's surface while staring straight ahead toward a stretch of sandy beach.

The speeding seaplane drops into the water with a jolting splash that sizzles off the smoking port-side engine. Alexa turns to Jimmy, bracing herself in her seat as she senses an imminent collision. She points forward out the window and cries, "Jimmy!!"

"Not now… Hold on!"

The damaged aircraft briefly eases down into the water and then quickly grinds up onto the beach with a spray of hard-packed sand. The pirate Catalina follows, with both engines roaring at full throttle. It quickly pulls up to avoid the dense wall of palm trees lining the shore.

Hands still holding onto the yoke, but to little effect, Jimmy tries to steer the speeding wreck as the stepped-hull carves its way through the sandy beach. He reaches up, pulls the throttle back on the remaining engine and cuts the fuel.

Wide-eyed, Alexa gasps as the beached seaplane races toward the impenetrable jungle. "Trees… Trees!"

Releasing his grasp on the useless controls, Jimmy braces himself, as sprays of beach flay out from the sliding hulk of metal. "I see 'em…"

The propellers continue to listlessly spin as sand shoots from the path of the crashing seaplane and the tree-line nears. With a gut-wrenching crunch, the seaplane hurtles into the trees, coming to an abrupt stop.

~*~

All is quiet, but for the hiss of cooling engines and the creak of twisted steel. Jimmy removes glass and broken branches from his lap and then looks over at Alexa slumped in her seat. He unbuckles his lap belt and moves next to her. "Alexa, are you okay?" He wipes the hair back from her face and gives her a tender kiss on the cheek. Touching his fingers to her slender neck, he feels for a pulse.

"C'mon darlin'…You're okay. Wake up."

A trickle of a smile crosses her lips, and she weakly opens her eyes. "That was a bit more than a rough landing."

Jimmy smiles as he pushes a palm frond away and unbuckles her harness. "Quint, you alive and okay back there?"

With a crash of dislodged gear and glass, Quint rises from the floorboards to stand and look at his bleeding leg.

"No… I'm shot in the leg."

"Again?"

"Nope. Same one… Still hurts."

"Let's get that bandaged up and get the heck out of here."

Slipping past Quint, Jimmy gives the sailor a pat on the shoulder. Followed by Curtiss, he moves into the cargo area. Alexa watches the pilot and copilot quickly exit and she touches the tender wound on her forehead. Her eyes meet Quint's, and she whispers, "Where are we going to go?"

"I was wondering the same thing."

~*~

The pirate Catalina flies past the beach and banks around toward the crash site. Dropping altitude, it flies low over the broken wreckage where the sand meets the trees. With guns aimed downward and ready, the menacing, warplane circles several times.

Inside the fuselage of the crashed seaplane, the shipwrecked crew silently listens to the drone of aircraft engines overhead. They hold their breath, taking note as the airplane covers the area and then flies off. Alexa looks questioningly to the others.

"Where are they going?"

Jimmy looks at the bullet-riddled fuselage and replies, "They will need repairs, before they can put down anywhere."

She puts her finger through a bullet hole in the bulkhead. "How are they going to do that?"

Quint smiles toward Jimmy. "They'll need to find a friendlier beach to land on."

Checking the load in his pistol, Jimmy pops the clip and slides the action back. He catches the ejected .45 auto round and thumbs it back into the nearly empty clip. He pulls a box of cartridges from the backpack and begins to reload. While reloading the clip, he glances up.

"We're on an island. They must figure we're not going anywhere, and we'll be here when they get back."

"Won't we be?"

Jimmy smiles at Alexa, as he slams the ammo clip back into the butt of his pistol. "Maybe, but we'll be ready for 'em." He looks over to Quint who nods in agreement, as he wraps clean bandages around his leg. Jimmy winces at the traces of blood soaking through the dressing. "You okay to walk?"

"It'll slow me down a bit, but I'll manage."

Jimmy opens a cabinet on the wall and grabs a stack of pistol and rifle ammunition boxes. "Let's get everything we need from here. Food, clothing, anything else we can use… then, we'll survey the island."

They raid the small pantry and Alexa loads a bag with supplies. Jimmy moves over to the arsenal of guns, grabs a Thompson machine gun from the rack and tosses it as he remarks to Quint. "Just like old times, eh?"

Quint catches the auto-rifle with a firm grip and sighs, "I was really enjoying my quiet, peaceful life before you stopped in for a friendly visit."

"We'll have you back there in no time."

"Preferably alive."

Jimmy smiles. "That's the goal."

Quint groans and shakes his head, as he loads the rifle. "With no more extra holes in me?"

"I never knew you to be so demanding."

"I'm getting cranky in my old age."

Jimmy tosses a few more boxes of rifle ammunition into the backpack and slides his arms through the shoulder straps. The boxes of cartridges rattle around as they settle inside. Quint stands, holding the machine gun, while testing his weight on the wounded leg. "Want me to carry something?"

Fastening a bag on her back, Alexa steps forward to grab a shotgun from the rack of weapons. She thumbs a few shells into the magazine, jacks the pump action, slamming a round into the chamber, and moves toward the side hatch. "Quint, just do what you can to keep up."

The two men look at each other, impressed by her skill and attitude. Quint cradles the Thompson automatic rifle under his arm and hobbles to the door. "Okay, let's get to it." Jimmy looks down to Curtiss and grabs hold of an outstretched hand. He gives his small friend an amenable shrug and follows the others outside.

Chapter 30

Marooned on one of the many uninhabited tropical islands in the South Pacific, Alexa finds it hard to not admire the picturesque beach with its wide, sandy shores and long, swaying palms reaching out from the jumble of vegetation. Alexa, following close behind Jimmy, looks back at Quint. They trek along the beach, hugging the tree-line, as Curtiss scurries in and out of the greenery.

Alexa catches up to Jimmy and looks around, amazed. "This place is beautiful."

"Yeah, we could stop for a vacation, if we didn't have people trying to kill us."

Limping along at the rear of the group, Quint grunts, "Usually ruins a good vacation."

Lines of sweat stream down Jimmy's temples, as he looks back at Quint. Taking a canteen from his bag, he takes a swig, and offers them some water. "Thirsty?"

Quint hobbles to catch up as Jimmy regards his bandaged friend. "Looks like you could use a vacation."

"Yeah... From the both of you."

As the humidity raises beads of sweat across Alexa's brow, she dabs it away with her shirtsleeve. After Quint hands her the canteen next, she takes a drink and then looks at his injuries. Coughing to cover her feelings of accountability, she hands back the canteen and trudges on. "C'mon boys... Let's keep moving."

Seemingly amused by this misadventure, Quint raises a bandaged brow and grins at Jimmy. Following Alexa's stoic example, he limps past him. "Yeah buddy, let's go."

~*~

Late in the afternoon, the party traveling the sandy beach comes to a long peninsula that juts out into ocean water. Jimmy leads the way, as they climb over the rocky arm of land that shelters a peaceful cove. He ducks hastily, crouching low, waiting for Alexa to catch up.

As Quint and Curtiss follow, Jimmy puts a shushing finger to his mouth. They all peer over the stone berm to see a lone, traditional Chinese sailing junk, sitting at anchor in the tranquil cove. Two small boats with oars have been pulled up onto the wide beach, where dozens of footprints lead into the dense jungle. Jimmy motions for everyone to keep down low as they scan the vacant beach. He whispers beside to the others, "I don't see anyone out there."

Quint removes a pair of binoculars from Alexa's pack and eases his head up just high enough to get a better look. "Me neither, but they won't be far."

"Gathering supplies, you think?"

Alexa turns to Quint. "Who are they?"

In unison, Jimmy and Quint mumble, "Pirates."

In shock, Alexa keeps her head concealed behind the ridge and speaks in a loud whisper. "More pirates! Do any normal people live here in the islands?"

Quint studies the sailing vessel and the beach near the boats. He sighs, then ducks back to cover and turns to his companions. "There are decent folk here, but they don't sail with cannons on their ship decks. Besides, it could be worse."

Astounded, Jimmy and Alexa both turn their attention from the cove to stare at Quint. Jimmy pulls Curtiss in close as Alexa asks the obvious. "How could it get worse?"

Quint shrugs, hands the pair of binoculars to Jimmy, and glimpses at them perceptively. "Believe me. It could…"

~*~

Where the beach meets the jungle, Jimmy and Alexa creep along the wall of vegetation. Quint and Curtiss follow, crouching low, moving their way toward the crew boats. Pausing, Jimmy puts his hand up to halt them in their tracks. He raises the binoculars and inspects the anchored sailboat. "There looks to be about three armed crew-members onboard. There's a swivel cannon on the poop deck and two large caliber defense guns, starboard and port."

Quint quietly whispers over Alexa's shoulder toward her ear, "I'd say they're definitely pirates."

"Maybe they're nice, civilized people needing to defend themselves *against* pirates."

Jimmy lowers the pair of binoculars and, with amusement, looks to Quint. He gestures toward the beached boats and smiles at Alexa while handing her the field glasses. "Would you like to try and have a talk with them first?"

"No… Not really…"

She takes the binoculars from Jimmy and scans the exotic sailing vessel. Her gaze travels to the boats on the sand. Speaking low as she holds the eyepieces to her face, Alexa asks, "What are we going to do? Steal one of those rowboats?"

Jimmy glances to Quint, who is crouched alongside. "What do you think? Could your sailing skills get us out of here in one of those?"

Quint shakes his head, doubtful. "We'd be pretty helpless in the open water with something small like that. Maybe I'd risk it if we had time to rig up a sail, and we didn't have people out to kill us."

Alexa hands the binoculars over to Quint, and he scans the area from the beached tenders outward. He pauses and studies the Chinese sailing junk and its twin-mast sail rigging. "Not much chance in the shore boats… We might in that bigger ship, though."

Turning from the sailor to the pilot, Alexa studies them to see if they're actually considering thievery on the high seas. "You mean, steal the *big* pirate ship? We can't do that!"

Jimmy whispers quietly, "It didn't bother you all that much when we took that pirate seaplane."

The idea of stealing from a larger group of pirates on the island seems to bother Alexa. "That happened in the heat of the moment."

Jimmy shrugs. "We're open to other ideas."

Lowering the field glasses, Quint flashes a roguish grin. "How do you think they got that boat in the first place?"

~*~

The three crouch low, crawling along the beach toward the unattended boats on shore. They stay close to the ground, using the beached vessels to block the view of the pirates aboard the sailing junk. Jimmy gets to one of the small boats first and takes cover against the hull, waiting for the others. They line up beside him, and Jimmy looks past Alexa to Quint and Curtiss. "We're only gonna take one of these boats. Check out the other one. Make sure it's seaworthy."

Alexa slides in next to Jimmy and peers over, as Quint crawls around to the other boat. "What are you going to do?"

"I'm going to make so this one won't float long."

Jimmy looks over the upturned hull and sees Quint nod his consent. Jimmy motions for him to get moving, and the old sailor starts pushing the wooden boat toward the surf. Alexa watches as Jimmy stabs his pocket knife in between the painted planks on the underside of the boat, working his thin blade into the seam. He looks up from the knife and smiles innocently at Alexa. "Take Curtiss and get into that other boat. Keep the guns low, out of sight, and I'll be along shortly."

"Do you want me to take the backpack?"

Jimmy presses on the knife blade, tilts his head and shakes it. "No. I'll be fine with it. Take both the Thompson rifles."

Alexa grabs the guns and moves around to the other boat, as Quint slides it along the beach. She looks back at Jimmy, still carving a hole in the hull of the first boat, and stashes the guns in the wood-slatted bottom of the other. Curtiss comes up from behind, and Alexa puts him into the boat before helping Quint push it into the shallow, ocean surf.

As the vessel begins to float, Alexa steps in and takes a seat near the rudder. Quint pushes the boat further into the water and stands knee-deep in the gentle rollers. He looks back to the other boat and quietly calls, "Come on, Jimmy... Time to go!"

Knife buried hilt deep, Jimmy finishes another gaping slit in the wooden underside of the boat. Jimmy looks up and waves them both on. He watches, as Quint gives another shove to the craft before leaping in and taking up the oars. Jimmy pulls his knife from between the painted slats, folds and pockets it. He glances to the island's tree-line before scurrying down the beach and sliding silently into the warm, rolling waves.

Jimmy swims behind the boat and clutches the stern. Quint, with his back to the bow, resumes his slow, steady rowing, toward the pirate ship. Jimmy clings alongside and whispers between oar strokes, "Have they seen us yet?"

Alexa fleetingly looks over the side at Jimmy, and then past Quint's rowing torso toward the waiting pirate ship. "Nothing yet. Where do you think they are?"

The experienced sailor pulls with steady strokes, barely making a splash with the oars, as the boat glides across the water's surface. He glances over his shoulder for reference and stays on course. "There is no reason for the crew on board to be watching the beach except, casual-like. The others are probably on the island scrounging for food and fresh water." Quint digs in and pulls with a long stroke of the wood oars. "There's a chance they saw or heard our airplane go down." He suddenly stops mid-row and lets the paddle blades drag.

The small boat continues to cut through the waves, drifting closer to the pirate sailing ship. Alexa looks at Quint strangely. "What is it, Quint?" The sailor peers over his shoulder and turns back to face Alexa, Curtiss and Jimmy. "If they've been here long, then Rasmus must have seen them, too."

Alexa gulps. "Which means?"

Jimmy pulls himself up behind the small boat, peeks over the stern toward the oriental sailing vessel and replies, "Rasmus sure won't be far behind, if he thinks someone else might get to us before he does."

There is commotion on the anchored pirate ship, followed by a loud blast of the cannon from the deck. Alexa watches as a whirling projectile splashes into the water a few yards from them. "Uh... they've seen us."

Curtiss crawls to the bottom of the small boat, between Quint's feet, and covers his furry hands over his eyes. Looking past his shoulder toward the pirate ship, Quint peeks over the side at Jimmy, across at Alexa and continues his rowing. "So much for the surprise attack."

Chapter 31

Three pirates, positioned on the deck of the Chinese junk, watch and wait. Two of the sailors hold machine guns at the ready, while another stands, above an unfurled rope ladder. Alexa watches, as a fourth pirate, behind the cannon, resets another charge. "Are we sure we want to do this?"

Quint looks at her peculiarly. "Is there another option we're not seeing?"

Still watching the pirates on the deck, Alexa shakes her head. "No, but this one isn't looking good."

He adjusts his grip on the oars. "How many?"

"It looks like four, and they all have guns."

Quint turns his effort back to the oars, continuing to row as Jimmy, hidden low in the water, holds on to the side of the boat. After another stroke of the oars, Quint looks down at Jimmy, across to Alexa and Curtiss, then over his shoulder. "What are they doing now?"

Alexa picks up Curtiss, as she stares toward the pirate vessel. "They're getting ready to shoot at us."

As the small boat gets closer to the pirate ship, Alexa moves Curtiss aside and stands to wave her hands in the air. "Don't shoot! Don't shoot..."

Holding his row, Quint watches her, slightly amused. "Hope they speak English."

The pirate crew watches tentatively as the small boat slowly glides to the side of their ship. Lowering their guns, they peer curiously at a bandaged, grey-haired man, and the pretty woman and monkey that accompany him. The rowed boat bumps the ship's hull under the dangling rope ladder. On her feet, Alexa smiles at them while waving cordially. "We need help. Do you understand?"

The greasy-haired pirate at the top of the ladder flashes a gold-plated, grin and gestures them aboard. Alexa glances at Jimmy, in the water, turns to Quint and smiles uncertainly. "They might be friendly after all."

Quint racks the oars, looks up at the long ammo magazine sticks protruding from the machine guns and then back to Alexa. "I doubt it, darlin'. Those weapons look none too friendly to me."

Alexa grabs the lower rungs of the rope ladder and begins to climb. Remaining hidden between the boat and the ship hull, Jimmy watches her climb. Quint holds it steady from below, glances overboard and ushers Curtiss after her.

~*~

On the ship deck, coming over the railing, Alexa is met by one of the pirates, his gun held ready against his shoulder. He jabs the barrel into her chest and prods her toward the mid-deck. She steps aside, as Curtiss climbs over the railing, followed by Quint.

Three of the pirates circle around their unexpected visitors. They mumble to each other in a native dialect, and, with narrowed eyes, examine the guests. Several terse phrases of the conversation are understood by Quint and he steps forward with his palms turned upward. He is instantly met with wide-eyed alarm and aggressive, pointed gestures with the automatic weapons. He steps back with his hands raised high in a calming gesture. "Whoa... Easy there..."

One of the pirates moves over to Alexa and pulls the bag from her shoulder. He reaches out, touches her light hair, and speaks to the others in a familiar Asian dialect. The crew laughs as Alexa, feigning a smile, rolls her eyes over to Quint. "What did he say?"

"You don't want to know."

When the pirate caresses Alexa's cheek, she swats his hand away. His mood quickly turns dark and he backhands her violently across the face, sending her reeling to the deck. Quint steps forward and is met with a jab to the abdomen with one of the rifles. Instantly, Curtiss jumps on the head of the nearest pirate and is promptly thrown across the boards.

A single, ear-splitting gunshot rings out. The pirate that threw Curtiss staggers back and slumps down against the main mast. Everyone turns to see Jimmy with his handgun still smoking as he rises from the side-rail. He wags his pistol at the remaining deck crew and swings a sopping wet leg over the handrail. "All right, that's enough..."

Dripping wet, Jimmy drops to the deck and leans back against the railing. "Are you okay, Alexa?"

Quint quickly grabs the nearest machine gun and then knocks the other rifles out of the hands of the pirates, as Alexa gets up, wiping a trickle of fresh blood from her busted lip. "I'm fine, Jimmy."

Jimmy looks up at the mast and then all around the top deck. "It looks like we have ourselves a boat."

He keeps his gun aimed at the pirates, as they stand staring with hostile intent. The seaplane pilot looks to his sailor friend and grins. "So Quint, can we sail this thing with just us three?"

Quint kicks the dropped guns aside and then inspects the sail rigging. "Not a problem, Jimmy."

"Good, then we won't be needing any of them around. Will you kindly escort them off the ship?"

His machine gun raised, Quint ushers the ship crew toward the side rail, giving one of the pirates a shove with the barrel of his gun. He speaks broken commands in an acquired Chinese dialect and the pirates shuffle toward the ship railing. As he moves the pirates across the deck, Quint throws a cunning wink to Alexa. "All right gentlemen, if you would, please step *to* the side and then *over* the side."

Quint barks another series of commands at the pirates. To add emphasis to his chopped vernacular, he gives the wounded crewman a push. The pirate looks away, then suddenly fills with terror. The pirates rush to the ship rails, and then they hastily dive over the side. Confounded by the sudden resolution to abandon ship,

Jimmy and Alexa step to the edge of the deck and watch as the terrified pirate crew swim to shore.

Jimmy looks at Quint. "What did you say?"

"Nothing that would cause them to do that."

A cold chill sweeps over them, as they suddenly recognize the familiar sound of radial airplane engines humming in the distance. Alexa clutches the side-rail and watches as the pirate seaplane emerges on the water from behind the jutting island peninsula. "Not again!"

A dropped rifle rattles unceremoniously to the wooden ship deck and Quint dashes to the starboard bow. "Jimmy, help me raise the anchor!"

Tucking his gun away, Jimmy follows after Quint. Alexa looks to the prowling warplane as it peeks over the coastline. "Can we outpace them on the water?"

Quint shakes his head at Alexa, as he strains against the turning reel of the anchor line. "Hell no!"

Grunting with effort, Jimmy waves Alexa over to help. "If we stay here, we're sitting ducks."

Alexa rushes to them, as the dripping anchor line slowly rises in the water. Several small caliber gunshots ring out from the shoreline. Jimmy stands upright to peer over the deck rail. He sees a row of Chinese pirates on the beach with guns aimed at the three strangers aboard the pilfered vessel.

Bullet hits plink around the ship's rigging, as Jimmy, muscles aching, ducks and continues to turn the anchor reel. "More pirates!"

The anchor finally clears the water. Quint secures it, before he bounds to the mast and begins to climb upward. "Jimmy, use the deck-gun to hold them off! Alexa and Curtiss, I need help to break out the canvas!"

Alexa gives Jimmy an astonished gaze. "For a roughed-up old fella, he's pretty nimble on a ship…"

Jimmy nods, "Certain death is a great motivator."

She follows after Quint, as Curtiss leaps to the rigging lines and climbs skyward.

~*~

Positioned behind the machine gun at the port bow, Jimmy pulls back the bolt, cocking the swivel-mount weapon. He points the gun toward the shore and squeezes the trigger in short bursts. Sand kicks up, as bullets shower the beach. The pirates dash for cover. Several of them race over to the remaining boat on the beach and push it into the rolling surf. Jimmy watches, as they row the boat out several yards before it fills with water. He laughs, as the angry pirates bail out of the boat and splash back to shore.

"That's it! Back to the beach with you all!" The deck-gun rattles and Jimmy riddles the beach again, sending the remaining pirates scurrying into the jungle.

High in the rigging, Quint and Alexa release the sails. The pleated canvas sheets spread out, snapping loudly as they billow in the wind. From their vantage, above the deck, they watch as Jimmy continues to fire short blasts toward the island, keeping the pirates at bay.

The drone of the pirate seaplane's engines catches Alexa's attention, and she turns to watch it, low in the water, finally coming around the peninsula. As it veers toward its stationary target, she notices the front hatch open over the nose position. "Jimmy, the seaplane!"

Jimmy sends one last barrage of bullets toward the beach and turns to the pirate Catalina in the water on the other side. "Dammit... They're here already?"

They watch as a lone air pirate emerges from the nose hatch of the seaplane with a mortar-style rocket launcher. Jimmy quickly jumps to the starboard deck-gun and pulls back the bolt. As the pirate takes aim at the ship, Quint yells down from the rigging. "Jimmy, take him out before he takes us out! A hit below the waterline and it's all finished!"

The ship's starboard deck-gun rattles loudly with a burst of gunfire. Jimmy gets off several rounds of ammo as the air pirate ducks and fires the rocket launcher. As if in slow motion, the projectile shoots out in a graceful, smoke-trailing arc toward the sailing junk. Seconds stretch as Jimmy watches, transfixed, before snapping out of his trance and diving away.

The rocketed mortar round sails through the clear blue sky and smashes into the starboard bow of the Chinese junk. The upper foredeck explodes, sending Jimmy, along with the mounted machine gun, flying. Tossed across the ship, Jimmy tumbles through a cloud of smoke and debris.

The seaplane draws nearer, and air pirates scurry onto the high wing, carrying machine guns and grappling hooks. Climbing down from the mainsail, Quint watches the side door on the seaplane swing open. A rubber raft is shoved out and dropped to the water. Several heavily armed pirates board it and make way for the sailboat.

Alexa steps around the debris on deck and uncovers Jimmy from the wreckage. She dusts him off, examining him for any injuries. Gunfire hails from the shoreline and Alexa pulls Jimmy to his feet and drags him from the broken mess. "You going to live?"

"Don't know yet."

"C'mon, I've put you through worse..."

Jimmy winces with pain, as she helps him gain his footing. "No... Things seem to be escalating."

Suddenly, Jimmy checks his shoulder and looks around, frantically, as if he's lost something. Alexa spots Curtiss hanging in the rigging, and she points to the monkey. "It's okay, Jimmy... Curtiss is right there."

He looks up, slightly relieved, but keeps searching. "Where's the backpack?"

Dropping to the deck from the main mast, Quint charges over and pulls the backpack out from under some debris. As the seaplane steadily approaches Quint tosses the bag to Jimmy. "Here it is," he blurts, as he peers over the side of the ship, "but I don't think that's the priority right now."

A grappling hook arches over the side rail and, with a grinding scrape, is pulled tight, locking into the ship deck. They watch as three more hooks follow in quick succession. Not yet steady on his feet, Jimmy grabs the backpack, slings it over his shoulder, and climbs the stairs to the poop deck.

"Cut those lines! Keep them from boarding."

Alexa watches him as he stumbles up the stairs. "Where are you going?"

Cresting the top of the stairway, silhouetted against the sky, he humorously turns to blow her a kiss. "Don't worry, sweetie! I'll be fine."

Alexa only has a second to be annoyed before Quint puts a sword in her hand and pulls her to the railing. "Hack those lines, while I try to hold 'em off."

Alexa chops at a tough grappling hook cord as the pirates in the raft toss several more over the rail. Quint finds a rifle on the deck, and he uses it to shoot several pirates as they climb over the side. As she cuts another line, Alexa assesses the increasingly overwhelming odds and turns to Quint. "What's he doing up there?"

Quint fires on another pirate who clings to the railing. "I don't know, but he better do it quick!"

As she holds the sword over her head, about to swing at another line, Alexa looks up toward the higher ship deck. "Hurry, Jimmy…"

The invading pirates swarm all around the deck, as Quint tosses an empty rifle away and grabs for another. The menacing rattle of cocking machine guns seems to come from all directions. Alexa waves the cutlass defensively, as she faces the boarding crew.

Chapter 32

High above the action mid-ship, Jimmy stands loading the aft cannon on the poop deck. He swivels the big gun and aims it down toward the cockpit of the pirate seaplane coming alongside in the water below. An explosion of wood splinters off the nearby railing and Jimmy turns to see an air pirate on the lower deck, firing his automatic rifle at him. He ducks aside and pulls his sidearm, firing several shots at the pirate. Safe for the moment, Jimmy tucks his pistol into his waistband and positions himself behind the deck-cannon again.

Jimmy howls with rancorous delight, as he aims the cannon down at the forward cockpit of the pirate seaplane. "Hey Captain Rasmus, put this in your pipe and smoke it!" Jimmy activates the trigger mechanism and the cannon blasts a whirling projectile into the front end of the seaplane. The cockpit and nose explode with the impact, and Jimmy watches as the whole aircraft structure rocks in the water and slowly sinks.

The hairs at the nape of Jimmy's neck tingle anxiously. He turns around to finds himself, once more, face-to-face with the air pirate captain - P. M. Rasmus.

The pirate's single, piercing blue eye shines out from below his grey fedora. He raises his pistol and aims it at Jimmy. "You will have to do much better than that to get rid of me, my fellow flyer. It will be my honor to return the pleasure." Jimmy stares down the pointed barrel of the Luger handgun, as he slowly moves astern. Rasmus follows, spitting his words with evil intent. "Captain Ferral, I believe I warned you not to get mixed up with that woman. My family line seems born to trouble and tragedy."

"I can see that now."

"A bit too late, wouldn't you say?"

"Ain't that the way with women?"

Jimmy raises his hands in surrender, as he backs against the wood railing of the high aft deck. The air pirate captain stops to examine Jimmy for a moment before reclaiming his calm, chilling charm. "You stole my moment of discovery... Where have you put the treasured headpiece? None of this rough play needs to go any further."

Like an innocent schoolboy, Jimmy grabs the wet leather straps of the backpack and hooks his thumbs behind. He offers a wry smile and shrugs. "It *was* pretty fancy... Appeared to be worth a few bucks... But it's gone now." Jimmy casts his eyes aside, looking for any means of escape. "It was because of one of your flunky pirates that it fell into a pit inside that island. I guess you didn't get the update?"

The fervent pirate leader shakes his head mournfully, and the muscles along his face ripple as he clenches his jaw. Without warning, Rasmus pulls the trigger. The bullet hits Jimmy in the fleshy part of his shoulder, directly through the strap of the rucksack.

Jolted back, Jimmy holds onto the railing and looks over at the precarious drop to the ocean below. He takes a quick breath and looks back to the intense stare of Rasmus. The pirate captain aims the smoking handgun at Jimmy's head and takes another step closer. "That had better be an embellishment of the truth, or you will experience more pain than you can even imagine. I want that treasure."

Jimmy glances again at the drop to the water below. Rasmus senses his plotting notion of escape and gives a laugh. "If you think you can swim your way out of here, you've gravely mistaken the situation. Either the sharks will suckle at your wound or you can join your forsaken pals on the beach... They *do* all seem eager to meet with you."

They both turn their gaze to the assembly of marooned pirates that continue to fire at the two intertwined water vessels as they drift slowly out of range. Rasmus lowers his voice, moving closer, keeping his pistol aimed at chest level. "Captain Ferral, you've brought ruination to my air-ships. Now, I will be taking over your newly acquired sea vessel."

Jimmy looks over at the blasted portion of the ship's foredeck and the half-sunken seaplane tethered alongside. He winces as he gestures with his injured arm. "Oh, this old thing? It's a bit of a fixer-upper."

"A comedian to the last. I will be very upset if I have to repeat myself. Now… Where is the headpiece?"

The skirmish of gunshots tapers off to an occasional isolated report from the beach. Jimmy rolls his shoulder under the bullet-pierced strap of the backpack and lightly touches the bloody wound underneath. A roguish glimmer flashes in the eyes of the injured pilot, as he looks down the end of the pirate captain's firearm. "Well, Capt'n, I guess we can do this the hard way."

Before Rasmus can blink an eye or squeeze the trigger, Jimmy flops back over the railing and ungracefully splashes into the clear blue seas below. Rasmus steps to the rail and peers down to the water, as Jimmy swims below the surface. He takes careful aim and fires several shots, until his gun finally clicks empty.

White channels of fizz follow the bullets as they whiz through the water and seem to bury themselves into their target. A trickle of blood taints the water and Jimmy's body sinks in a halo of bubbles, disappearing under the ship's hull. Rasmus offers a salute of his firearm before ejecting the empty clip and slapping a fresh one in. "Goodbye, Captain Ferral. Consider it a professional courtesy that I let you off so easily."

~*~

Several cautious air pirates hang onto grappling lines, guns at the ready, waiting for the right opportunity to board. The rest of the pirate aircrew flees from the sinking seaplane, severing any remaining tethers as they go. On the main deck, Quint and Alexa face off with the few remaining air pirates attempting to take the vessel. Alexa holds a handgun and aims it at a pirate coming over the rail. It clicks empty, and she stumbles back into Quint. "I'm out of ammunition."

Quint looks down at the empty chamber of the rifle in his hands. "Yeah. Me too…"

They both backpedal across the deck, and air pirates ascend the railing. As the pirates advance on them, Alexa hollers over her shoulder toward the stern of the ship. "Jimmy! We need some help down here!" Her gaze travels up the stairway to the upper deck.

The high midday sun silhouettes the dark, menacing figure of Rasmus at the upper-deck rail. "I am sorry my dear, but you'll have to settle for me instead."

Alexa feels a gripping wave of dread sweep over her, as she catches the evil smile that lingers on the captain's shadowed features. Then, Quint turns to confront the few remaining pirates, as they slowly advance with guns aimed at the both of them. He drops his weapon to the deck with a clanking thud and raises his hands up in surrender. "Huh? Only five of you left? We *almost* got you all…"

One of the air pirates steps forward and swings the butt of his rifle across Quint's temple, knocking him out cold. Alexa turns as her battered friend crashes to the deck. The pirate turns his weapon toward her, and she quickly drops her firearm at his feet. She raises her hand, shrugging innocently. "We give up."

Surrounded by battle-angered buccaneers, Alexa glimpses up toward her overseeing uncle. With the pleated canvas sails flapping idly behind him, the air pirate captain looms over them all. Alexa evaluates the dire situation and releases a pained sigh of exhaustion.

Chapter 33

The Chinese sailing junk travels through the rolling ocean swells with a full spread of its exotic patterned-canvas sails. Piles of debris from the mortar blast are stacked against the bow on the port side. The rest of the deck has been cleared. The pleated sail-rigging creaks, as it pulls the vessel westward with a turned swale of clear, blue sea following in the wake.

Inside the captain's quarters, Rasmus sits in an ivory-carved chair, fiddling with his leather eyepatch. He looks at the ocean view through the bay windows, and turns to observe the cabin's lavish accommodations. He glimpses to where Alexa sits in a nearby chair, as he twirls his finger through some fine silk drapery.

"This band of celestial misfits seems to have done well for themselves. Too bad they're out of business now and left to play patty-cake for the duration."

Rasmus flips open the lid of a carved box that sits on the table next to him. A pointed finger idly stirs its contents of precious stones. He selects one and holds it up in the sunlight.

"They have acquired some valuables and more than a few artifacts that you might be interested in."

Alexa looks down to Quint laid out on the floor, bloody and unconscious, and then looks over to the armed pirate henchman at the door. She watches, as Rasmus rolls the gem between his thumb and finger, admiring the refracted light. The enigmatic air pirate captain examines the cut and purity, and then looks to her with a probing eye. "You and your new associate, the navy flyer, turned out to be quite the nuisance. He has cost me a lot of resources. Not to mention the number of men I'll have to replace…"

"There always seems to be available pirates."

"Yes, but my crew require a unique set of skills."

"Maybe you should retire? Find a nice spot on the beach and hang up your eye patch…"

Rasmus' single eye narrows with a glare of indignation. "Under different circumstances, he would have been a valuable asset to me. The two of you could have enjoyed the lifestyle of true treasure hunters and profited as well."

"What do you want from me? An apology?"

With a clink, the jewel is dropped back into the chest. After a long, quiet pause, Rasmus angrily swats the box aside, crashing it against the wall and scattering its contents across the floor. He turns to Alexa and bears down on her with his singular penetrating eye and dark, leather eyepatch. "You don't seem to understand, Alexa. Your life, as well as the life of your companion here, is dependent on my receiving that headpiece. Do you want to follow your friend, Captain Ferral, to a watery grave?"

At the mention of Jimmy's demise, she sits back firmly in the chair, trying to keep her composure. She stares ahead at her uncle in the carved throne, and shakes her head. "It's the fault of your slash-happy pirates that our treasured headpiece will be forever lost inside that island."

The pirate captain grips the arms of the chair and rises to his feet, standing silhouetted against a panel of windows. Alexa squints into hazy beams of sunlight and finds that she is once more trying to interpret her uncle's angry expression. The ship rocks gently and Rasmus takes a calming breath before walking toward Alexa.

He circles her seated position like a predatory animal, then stops to look down at Quint, unconscious on the floor. Dissatisfied, he shakes his head as he contemplates the unconscious sailor, and then moves to confront Alexa. Bending down some, Rasmus looms over his estranged niece. "I *will* have that headpiece, damn you! Do you realize how much you have cost me? Forget the air-ships and the men... My time and reputation are worth much, much more."

Staring back at him like an insolent child, Alexa shrugs. "Want me to write you a check?"

Rasmus lunges forward and grabs her around the neck. His strong hands wrap tightly around her slender throat and squeeze tightly. "No... I want that crown!"

Alexa gasps for air as she claws at his clenched fingers, trying to loosen his grip.

~*~

The junk, with its mortar-smashed starboard bow, moves along with the sails in full-spread. Near the broken heaps of wood and rope-rigging piled on the deck, a wet, shaking hand reaches up to grab hold of the damaged railing.

Pale and water-soaked, the hand pauses for a moment. It is soon followed by the ragged, near-drowned seaplane pilot, still wearing the bullet-torn backpack. He crawls up through the broken railing beneath the jib sail and slides onto the foredeck. Concealed amongst the debris, he heaves a heavy sigh of exhaustion.

~*~

The enraged air pirate captain stands over Alexa, as she struggles for air. He finally releases the grip on her throat and leaves her gasping for breath. Rasmus rubs his palms together and smooths his fingers over the reddened scratches on his wrists and hands. He walks to the wide panel of windows and stares, reminiscently, out over the expansive of vacant sea.

"Call it family intuition, but I still think you're lying. Your father was also often stubborn and foolish. It was his insolence that forced my hand."

Rasmus pauses and steals a glance over his shoulder to observe Alexa's reaction. As her panting eases, resentment wells up inside her. The knuckles gripping the arms of her chair turn white, and she watches the suggestion of a smile cross the pirate's lips. Rasmus turns back to the ocean view and continues, "We were inseparable best friends as children. It wasn't until it was too late that he realized that familial ties only stretch so far... We will see if you are cursed to follow in his footsteps."

Rasmus pulls his jacket aside and draws his Lugar pistol from the shoulder holster nestled under his arm. Determined, the interrogator walks over to where Quint lies, unconscious, on the floor. Standing over the prone figure, the malevolent uncle looks to Alexa while cocking his firearm. "Your new associate is about to die for your expedition. Anything you would like to say to me now?"

Alexa clenches her teeth. She looks down at Quint stretched out on the floor with his head slumped to the side, oblivious to the imminent danger. She looks back up to see the brother of her father, ready to pull the trigger. Raw emotion shows on her face, as she silently stares ahead, tears welling up in her eyes.

Unwavering, Rasmus glares at her and waits for an answer. "My girl, you are hard to be friends with."

A teardrop rolls down Alexa's cheek. "I told you already... *I don't have it.*"

"But, can you take me to where it is?"

"I can show you where it *was.*"

Rasmus thinks, then nods approvingly and lowers the aim of his pistol. "That's the family spirit."

~*~

With a pirate in the rigging and another midship, gazing toward the horizon, the sailing vessel appears to be almost empty. Wood planks creak softly, as Jimmy creeps across the deck, moving to the back of the ship. He stops, and waits at the hallway entrance under the stairs leading to the captain's quarters.

At the end of the corridor, with a Thompson machine gun propped against the wall, a pirate stands posting guard. Jimmy pauses to consider his plan of attack. Turning his attention to a shuffle of boots on deck, he is suddenly slammed into the adjacent wall by a pirate coming up behind. Held by his backpack, Jimmy clumsily swings an arm back at his attacker. His bent elbow clubs the assailant in the ear and the crewman yelps in pain.

They struggle for a rifle slung on the pirate's shoulder, as they slam each other against the underside of the stairway. The other guard rushes down the hall and aggressively points his machine gun at Jimmy. "Drop it, or I'll shoot you both!"

As the first pirate turns to his comrade with a look of disbelief, Jimmy releases his grip on the pirate's gun. With hands raised, he smiles innocently. "Nice to see you all again."

~*~

From inside the captain's quarters, Rasmus hears the commotion on deck. He looks to the guard in front of the closed door. "What's going on out there?"

The pirate tries to listen through the door and returns the captain's query with an unknowing shrug. Angered, Rasmus raises his gun at the man, hissing, "Don't stand there, stupid. Go and find out!" The air pirate opens the door and steps back to reveal Jimmy standing at the threshold, dripping-wet, with both arms raised in surrender.

Alexa blinks away her tears, "Jimmy!"

With his lone eye staring wide open, Rasmus gawks in disbelief at the resurrected pilot. Lowering his gun slightly, he squints at the figure he sees before him. "You again?"

Jimmy lifts his shoulders. "Not bad for one eye."

Rasmus' temper flares, as he raises his gun and fires at the doorway. Jimmy lunges to the side and drops down as the bullet tears into the pirate standing behind. The unsuspecting crewman staggers back and slumps in the hallway.

Jimmy grabs for the fallen pirate's gun and pulls it free. He racks the rifle's bolt and dashes down the hall passageway. Firing several rounds at the crewman at the hallway entry, Jimmy looks back as the other pirate slams the main cabin's wooden door shut.

Taking advantage of the distraction, Alexa swings a fist around and slugs Rasmus on the temple. He flinches, and she knocks the gun from his hand and kicks it across the floor. Rasmus slaps her down, and they briefly grapple for the loose gun, before he overpowers her and throws her from his path. With a thud Alexa tumbles across a table and into the wall.

As Rasmus reaches for his pistol on the floor, he sees a small, furry hand grab for it first. He looks up to see Curtiss, holding the handgun out provokingly. "Damn rodent, come here!" Rasmus lunges for his gun, as Curtiss scampers away, still clutching the firearm.

~*~

Tucked into one of the chamber door-pockets, mid-hallway, Jimmy reaches out and returns gunshots to the air pirate at the entrance to the captain's quarters.

They exchange fire, until two more pirates appear at the hallway beneath the stairs. Jimmy considers his blocked escape route and pulls back into the recessed cubby. "Jeez, they're like roaches."

The trapped pilot keeps his body tucked back, as he hides from the barrage of bullet-lead flying in both directions. He watches as the wooden wall panels near him splinter and tear apart, mere inches from his body. The narrow length of corridor fills with the thundering staccato of dueling Thompson machine guns and the pungent smell of spent black-powder smoke.

Chapter 34

Sunlight filters through a haze of acrid gun-smoke in the captain's quarters. Rasmus corners Curtiss and threateningly reaches out for the furry copilot. Behind him, spent brass cartridges fly through the doorway, as the crewman unloads his forty-five caliber Thompson auto-rifle into the hallway. Just as Rasmus lunges for Curtiss, the monkey drops the pistol and leaps to the safety of the thick curtains.

Rasmus quickly scoops up his handgun and turns to face Alexa. As he pivots, an antique cutlass hammers down on his wrist, knocking the firearm loose and across the floor. Alexa raises the heavy weapon again, as Rasmus hugs his bleeding hand to his chest while uttering curses under his breath. In pain-filled wrath, he glares at Alexa and advances toward her.

"Deary, what the hell do you think you are going to do with that old-fashioned sword? You can barely lift it to swing, let alone defend yourself." He steadily moves

toward her, cradling his cut wrist. He smiles, as she
sluggishly brandishes the large sword before her.

~*~

Bullets hammer into the walls, whizzing past as
Jimmy stays tucked in the narrow cubby. He flattens
himself against the chamber door and bides his time,
until there is a lull in the gunfight as the pirates reload.
Summoning a dose of courage, he takes a breath and
throws himself across the hall for a clear shot at the
single pirate at the main quarter's entrance.

He unleashes a burst of fire that catches the pirate
at the entryway across the knees. Ducking back across
again, Jimmy clings to the door as the reloaded pirate
opposite opens fire with his machine gun. The
overexcited air pirate hits everything in sight, including
the wounded pirate hunkered down by the captain's
cabin doorway.

After the violent hail of bullets, a cloud of gun-
smoke rolls through the hallway and the shooting stops
momentarily. The remaining pirate reloads his clip of
ammo and moves slowly down the hallway. When he
reaches the mid-corridor door pocket, where Jimmy was
hiding, he swings around the corner, and a burst of hot
lead spews from his weapon.

The pirate faces an empty space with a bullet-
riddled cabin door before him. As the smoke clears, the
pirate kicks the narrow door open and peers inside. Ears
ringing in the silence, he listens intently and then directs
a burst of gunfire toward the bunks stacked against the
wall. "Come on out! Where are ya?" He studies the small
room and looks up to the open porthole window.

The pirate steps up on a wooden bunk and points the smoking-hot barrel of his rifle out through the open window. He pushes the gun farther outside, and then he pokes his head and shoulders out for a better look. Holding the rifle while twisting at the waist, he scans the hull and then the entire length of the ship.

Jimmy lunges from behind the shattered door, grabs the pirate by the ankles, and heaves him the rest of the way out through the porthole window. There is a brief wailing scream, quickly followed by the splash of the rifle and then a much larger splash as the gunman hits the water. Delighted, Jimmy quickly peers outside to watch, as the crewman surfaces once before disappearing in the sailing ship's wake.

~*~

Rasmus corners Alexa in the cabin, as she waves the heavy sword defensively. He swoops in and out, like a predator, toying with its prey. When she tires from her effort to wield the cumbersome sword, Rasmus pounces to grab the cutlass from her hands.

He tosses the blade away, which clatters to the floor, and holds Alexa tightly with both of his hands. Blood flows from the slash on his wrist, dripping down his arm to stain his crème-colored coat, as he looks intently into Alexa's eyes. Overwhelming fear fills her whole being, as the pirate's single eye seems to penetrate right through her as it dances with psychotic glee

When the cabin door smashes open, Rasmus and Alexa turn to see the unfailing seaplane pilot bound into the room. Jimmy quickly assesses the situation and snaps off a shot from his handgun. The pirate captain flinches away as the bullet smashes high into the cabin wall near his right shoulder. Adjusting his aim, Jimmy calls out, "Hey Rasmus! We're not through yet!"

The pirate captain spins toward Jimmy, and Alexa tries to pull free from his grasp. He violently grabs her by a fistful of hair and jerks her closer to him. Rasmus wraps his free hand around Alexa's bruised neck, and takes a firm hold. "Drop the gun, flyboy, or all I have to do is squeeze."

Jimmy hesitates. "You wouldn't hurt her."

"And why is that?"

Jimmy keeps his gun raised while he studies the desperate pirate leader. "She's family?"

Smiling wickedly, Rasmus places his chin on her trembling shoulder and turns her face to look toward Jimmy. He whispers to them both, "You should have seen what I did to her father…"

Immediately, Jimmy steadies his aim and squeezes the trigger of his handgun. He gasps at the faint click of a misfire. The two men stare at each other briefly, until their gaze drops to the loose German pistol on the floor, between them. Simultaneously, they dive for the firearm.

In short order, both men have a grip on the Luger pistol. Rasmus and Jimmy struggle on the floor, vying for control of the handgun. They roll across the cabin, smashing everything in their path, until Rasmus gets the upper hand by pressing a stiff thumb into Jimmy's fresh shoulder wound. With a howl, Jimmy grimaces in pain, as he tries to keep away from the pointed barrel of the deadly weapon.

Rasmus stabs his thumb into Jimmy's wound again and sneers vehemently, "I'll be sure to kill you this time." The two grunt with exertion. Jimmy tries to push back, as Rasmus slowly overpowers him, gaining control of the gun. A wicked smile stretches across the lips of the one-eyed pirate, as his face trembles with murderous effort. "Farewell, Captain Ferral..."

A sickening crack resembling the splitting of a melon freezes time for an instant. Rasmus' head jerks with a stiff jolt and his single eye opens wide. The black leather eyepatch tumbles free to reveal a scarred, empty socket beneath.

Still holding his breath, Jimmy looks up from the business end of the Luger to see the tip of the cutlass blade protruding over the top of the pirate captain's head. He twists the barrel of the pistol away from his face and pulls it from the captain's grip. Shocked, Jimmy exhales loudly before darting his eyes toward Alexa.

Alexa stands over the two tangled bodies on the floor. She holds the heavy pirate cutlass out from her waist, firmly gripped with both hands. Numbly, she looks down at the steel blade solidly embedded in the top of her uncle's head.

Jimmy rolls out from under the dead pirate and tosses the pistol aside. He removes Alexa's hands from the sword, and embraces her tightly. "Are you all right?"

Alexa trembles in Jimmy's arms and glances down at her uncle. "Not really... Are you?"

The two survivors spring back to action at the sound of a cough and a drawn-out moan. Alexa reaches for the gun and Jimmy yanks the bloody cutlass from

Rasmus' skull, and the body falls limp on the cabin floor. Jimmy brandishes the sword in defense, as he pushes Alexa around and behind him. The old pirate cutlass in hand, he slowly scans the room for an unseen aggressor.

On the floor, Quint rolls over slowly and sits up, cradling his battered temple. Dazed, he stares at Jimmy, holding a sword at the ready, with Alexa peeking out from behind him. After a moment, he breaks into a smile and asks, "Gee… Did I miss the party?"

Chapter 35

As a warm afternoon breeze blows steadily across the south sea waters, it lays a slight tinge of salt on uncovered skin. Under full canvas, the Chinese sailing junk cuts through the waves, as the descending sun shoots brilliant colors through clouds on the horizon. At the stern on the upper deck, Jimmy and Alexa sit near each other. They seem a comical expression of battle fatigue, with wounds and lacerations wrapped in makeshift dressings.

The two gaze out over the vast, surrounding seascape, lost in the wind-swept stillness. Curtiss pops his furry head up from below and peels back his lips in a toothy grin. Startling them both, he wears Rasmus' black leather eyepatch draped over one side of his face. Alexa ducks away and hides her face on Jimmy's shoulder.

"Curtiss! That's terrible."

Quint appears on the laddered-stairway and rolls them a dark, uneven-shaped bottle. The squat glass jug wobbles toward them across the planks of the wooden deck. Jimmy stops it with his hand, sets it upright, and asks, "What's this?"

"I think it's supposed to be wine. Try it."

Jimmy tugs the cork out and raises the bottle to his lips. Quint watches, as Jimmy swallows, gives a convulsive shiver and passes it to Alexa. She takes a tiny swig, and Quint grins through his bruised features. "That's just *some* of the good stuff I found in the galley."

Adorned with a fresh application of bandages, Quint takes in the ocean view, and then looks at Jimmy and Alexa. He smiles astutely. "Don't know exactly where the *Pirate-Pleasure-Cruise* is bound, but should be there in a week or so."

After taking another short swig from the bottle, Alexa lets the warm burn of the intoxicating brew sweep over her. She suddenly feels self-conscious and eases away from Jimmy. While kindly assessing his injuries, Alexa smiles at Quint. "Thank you for everything."

Standing on the stairs, Quint gives a flourishing salute. "At your service, ma'am."

"I'm sorry about your..." She gestures sympathetically to Quint's bandaged features, but he shrugs it off.

"All in a day's work running with Jimmy, there."

Enjoying the effects of the drink, Alexa takes another swallow from the bottle. Her eyes flutter toward Jimmy, and she grins sweetly. "He does tend to make life more difficult."

She passes the bottle to Jimmy, as Quint shakes his head, laughing. "I had a relaxing lifestyle on my peaceful little island, until our flyer pal here shows up in his seaplane with tales of treasure, damsels in distress, and perilous pirates."

Jimmy takes a coughing swallow from the dark jug and tilts his head in disbelief. "I had a pretty good setup myself, before she arrived."

Alexa and Quint exchange an understanding glance. Up in the sail rigging, a solitary bird catches the fury copilot's attention, and he scurries off along the top of the handrail. Through his facemask of bandages, Quint winks at Alexa. "Some folks just don't know when they got it good."

Jimmy grudgingly observes, as his old friend manages to charm all her attention at his expense. Low at his side, out of sight from Alexa, he gives Quint a brief, shooing wave. With a crafty twinkle in his eyes, the old sailor tosses his long strands of gray hair away from his face and tucks them behind his ears. He glances toward Jimmy as the pilot shoots him a familiar frown. "What's the funny look for, pal?"

"Are you sure you're feeling all right, Quint? Those bandages look like they need some attention."

Quint wobbles his head in mock disgust, as his fingertips trace the bandaged sutures along his cheeks. "Jimmy, you never fail to abuse me." Quint grins, and descends the ladder-style stairs to the lower deck. "Yes, yes... There are many things to attend to on my new sailing vessel. Bullet holes, explosions, blood stains..."

Alexa turns her gaze upward to the billowing sails. "Well, Jimmy, I guess it's not all a complete loss... We didn't recover the treasure, but Quint came out with a much larger boat." Her bright eyes remain skyward, transfixed by the vision of wind in the rolling canvas. "What's he going to do with a sailing ship like this?"

"Sell it or trade it. That's what he does."

"Where do you sell a shot-up pirate ship?"

"Either this port or the next. There always seems to be someone with cash on the barrelhead in Quint's circles." Jimmy studies Alexa's upturned face, as she stares aimlessly. "Are you okay about your uncle?"

Alexa shudders, and Jimmy places a calming hand to her arm. She glimpses at him, then resumes her upward gaze. "I don't even want to think about him." She closes both her eyes a moment, as she muses over some childhood memories. "When I was younger, I thought he only existed in scary stories told to naughty children. Many years later, I was doing research out here in the islands, and I heard his name mentioned again, in passing, but I never really believed he existed."

Jimmy smooths his hand over Alexa's shoulder, near the fresh bruises on her neck. He looks to her with a puzzled expression. "You didn't even know Rasmus before you got me mixed up in all of this?"

She turns to look at Jimmy, realizing the implications. "No more than you did." A cool breeze shifts across the deck, and Alexa hugs her shoulders tight. She then reaches over to Jimmy's bandaged hand and gives it a comforting squeeze. "Actually, you officially met him before I did. I was stashed in the compartment of your seaplane, remember?" With an understanding nod, Jimmy laughs to himself as he reaches for the nearby, bullet-riddled backpack.

"I have something for you…"

"What is it, Captain?"

Jimmy digs around the inside of the canvas bag and pulls one of her skimpy undergarments from the duffle. He mock examines it with approval and tucks it back before continuing the search. "That's not it."

Feeling around, his hand touches something and a slow smile spreads over his face. Alexa watches him inquisitively, as he slowly draws his arm from the backpack. His hand stops just inside the opening of the canvas flap.

"Close your eyes."

"Really, are you serious?"

Jimmy smirks. "Yeah, just do it."

A chill of nervous excitement shivers through Alexa as she watches Jimmy's restrained enthusiasm. "Okay Captain, but it better be good."

"Have I *ever* disappointed you?"

Alexa grimaces, as she covers her hand over her face. He carefully takes out the jeweled headpiece and places it gently on her lap. She instantly opens her eyes and smiles, both shocked and confused. "It's beautiful."

Lost in thought, she examines the treasure's details while mentally referring to her extensive notes. Smoothing her hand over the inlaid jewels, she rubs them with her fingertips. "It could use a cleaning."

Alexa looks at Jimmy enjoying her delighted reaction. "How did you…?

"It's just a little something I held on to."

"You had it all this time?"

He shrugs, as she reaches out, grabs hold of his collar, and jerks him close. She stares into his eyes. Her tone is playful, yet tinged with underlying seriousness. "You've been keeping this from me, Captain Ferral?"

"I wasn't sure how things would play out."

They lock eyes in a lengthy stare, each unsure of the other's next move. The joyful excitement in her eyes seems to override her conflicted feelings, and she forgives everything. She looks down at the headpiece and a smile crosses her lips. "By the way, how do you think things are turning out?"

"Better..."

"I can't believe you saved this."

With faces held close enough to sense her sweet breath, Jimmy smugly smiles. "That's what you pay me for, isn't it?"

"You deserve a raise..."

"What about Quint?"

"He got a boat."

He grins, as she pulls him in for a kiss, and they lock in an amorous embrace. The two cling together passionately. Oblivious to their surroundings, Jimmy and Alexa ease down to the wooden planks of the deck and push everything aside.

As Jimmy positions his arms around her, he bumps the headpiece from her lap, and it rolls off onto the ship's deck. With each of their complete attention focused on the other, they fail to notice, as the jeweled headpiece begins to wobble and roll away. Slowly, it travels toward the edge of the ship's railing and the heaving, blue seas below.

In the warm, afternoon breeze the Chinese pirate junk continues to sail through the pink-hued, reflected waters of the South Pacific, toward the blazing light of the setting sun.

The End . . .

. . . But then, sometime later . . .

A ruin of a decaying fortress lies concealed in the vegetation of a tropical forest in Southeast Asia. A sliver of evening sunlight streams through the tiny windows of a stone room. Jimmy, sweat-stained and mud-smeared, stares across the room toward a female archeologist as she the reads ancient passages carved into the walls of the stone chamber.

The robust entry door rattles open and an armed guard stands silhouetted in the threshold. He motions with the shaft of his primitive spear, and Jimmy rises to his feet. Briefly, the two adventurers turn to look to each other questioningly. Alexa gives a feeble shrug, as Jimmy shakes his head with practiced annoyance. He ushers her toward the exit with a sweeping bow.

~*~

The white-and-blue amphibious seaplane flies low over narrow waterway straights that separate clumps of jungled isles. The rumbling of its radial engines reverberate across the rippling ocean waves, sending flocks of waterfowl into flight. At the controls of the flying boat, Cutter, gripping the yoke, clenches a half-smoked cigar in his teeth.

With a shuddering roar, the plane veers close to one of the small islands and Cutter looks over to the copilot's seat. Curtiss leaps from Quint's lap and scurries to the cargo hold, leaving the long-haired sailor, white-faced, gripping the frame of the chair. Quint casts a wary eye to Cutter at the controls. "Thought you said this would be a simple pick up and go?"

Cutter flashes a toothy grin around the chomped cigar and grimaces. "He's hooked up with that treasure-digger gal. It's never uncomplicated when you have a woman involved, especially that one!"

The high-winged seaplane skims low over the ocean swells, as it swerves between the islands. As the plane disappears into a bank of fog, the sound of the twin radial engines slowly fades away.

~*~

Alexa Reid, University of Chicago – 1939

The large trees and trimmed lawns of the college campus are in full green as a cool breeze blows in off Lake Michigan. Clusters of students scramble between the old buildings, clutching their books, hoping to make it to their class on-time. A striking, long-haired woman, Alexa Reid makes her way out of the Oriental Institute. At the base of a flight of stairs, she is met by a professor dressed in a three-piece tweed suit. The older gentleman leads her short distance away from a crowd of students waiting to cross the street and speaks to her in a secretive tone, "I received a letter from your father."

At the mention of her father, a look of nervous excitement lights up her features. "When did it arrive?"

The scholarly gentleman holds up his leather briefcase and touches it with his hand, as he bends his head to the side. "I found it in my stack of mail today and came to find you... Let's walk."

He adjusts the brim of his fedora covering his salt-and-pepper hair, as they stride away from the university building. Professor Nathan J. Brunnabend has been an instructor at the school for several decades and is now the department head, overseeing research work at Chicago House in Luxor, Egypt. His confident stride and nimble manner offsets his academic attire. At his heels, Alexa follows him across University Street, seeming very much like a pupil keeping up with her teacher.

Slowing his pace as they reach the expansive lawns and keyhole-shaped walkways of the campus quadrangle, Professor Brunnabend lingers as Alexa maneuvers through a cluster of students to regain her spot at his side. He utters softly, "The postmarks were from Germany..."

He quickly glimpses around at the sea of innocent young faces that make their way between the gothic-style buildings. "What have you heard from your father lately?" Alexa notices the professor's apprehension as she answers, "Nothing since he left over a month ago."

The professor tilts his head and Alexa continues to follow him along the angled pathway through campus. Walking beside the briefcase, that swings like a pendulum, at the older man's side, she leans in close as he speaks to her. "The most recent telegram I received was from Berlin. He said he was planning to travel outside the city to follow a lead about smuggled artifacts appropriated from Egypt." He glances at her and continues, "It seems likely that there will be another war in Europe very soon. He stated that the tension in the region is overwhelming and the sense that something is about to happen is at the forefront of everyone's mind."

Alexa appears concerned, as she and the professor continue to walk down the pathway that leads through the well-tended campus gardens. A group of students breaks them apart momentarily as they cut through, and Alexa jogs a step to regain her position. "Did he say what the chances were for recovery or when he would return stateside this time?"

The professor shakes his head, as he veers off to the assembly of buildings along the southern perimeter of the walking path. "I hadn't received another communication from him until I received a package on my desk this morning."

"What was in it?"

The professor doesn't answer, but instead seems to clutch the handle of his briefcase tighter, quickening his pace. Alexa follows him on the paved walkway, around the corner and toward the Harper Memorial Library on 59th Street. Without questioning him further, she follows him up the steps and into the building.

Inside the library, Professor Brunnabend strides past several groups of studying students, until he comes to an empty table. He gestures for Alexa to take a seat and slides into a chair opposite from her. Leaning forward on the table, he softly whispers. "I know you must have a lot of questions." She quietly nods her head and watches, as the professor scans the faces of the people in the room.

The professor appears, at least momentarily, satisfied as to their privacy, and he lays his briefcase on the tabletop. He places his hand on the clasp and stares at her. "Your father is not only an accomplished archeologist…" Alexa nods her head and responds. "Yes, I know. I hear he is quite the popular instructor when he shows up for classes."

Professor Brunnabend bows his head down with an acquiescent gesture, "Yes, popular because of his lifestyle outside the academics."

Alexa looks at the professor's hand protectively placed on the cover-flap of the briefcase. "What is it you wanted to show me professor?"

The professor resumes the secretive conversation. "How well you know your father and his career?"

Alexa seems a somewhat annoyed and responds, "Traveling with him at a young age and then not seeing him again for twelve years, I would say, 'not at all' would be a massive understatement."

The professor nods, as he unfastens the clasp of the briefcase. "Yes, I realize that your personal reconnection with him all started with your time here at the university."

"After he abandoned me for his mission in China, nobody even knew if he was still alive."

"Unfortunate, yes...Regrettable, most definitely."

"What is it you're trying to tell me, professor?"

Reaching inside the briefcase, the professor takes out a tattered envelope stamped with post markings from Europe. He opens the letter and reads over the first few sentences before placing it on the tabletop and turning it toward Alexa. She lowers her gaze to read the handwritten message and, after a minute, looks back up to the professor.

"What package is he referring to?"

The professor reaches inside his case again and brings out a brown, paper-wrapped bundle the size of a small book. Alexa looks at the old professor inquiringly, and she asks, "Have you opened it?"

"No, I thought that would be for you to do."

He slides the wrapped parcel across the table to her while scanning the library again, determined to keep their exchange private. Alexa examines the marks on the package. Her eyes turn to the professor. "A book?"

"That is what it appears to be."

"Should I unwrap it now?"

The professor nods and takes the letter from the table, folds it over and slides it back into the envelope. "From what he penned in the message, I would say so. Go ahead." He puts the letter back in his briefcase but keeps the flap open. "I do have something else for you, later…"

Alexa nods and unfolds the paper-wrapped package. She takes out a leather-bound journal with a string-wrapped closure. The initials *AR* are embossed on the fold-over flap. She looks up at the professor quizzically and wonders aloud, "It's not even my birthday. Not that he would know when that was…"

"A gift is a gift."

She carefully undoes the leather tie and opens the book. Flipping through the journal, she is greeted by multiple pages of plain, ivory-colored paper. She appears very disappointed. "He sent me an empty journal of his travels?"

The professor leans forward, watching curiously as she flips through the blank pages. Suddenly his hand darts out, and his index finger catches one of the pages near the cover. "It says something…"

Alexa looks down to the page. He takes his hand away, as she flips to the previous blank page and then back again to a handwritten inscription:

For an educated traveler and scholar…
Here is a place to keep your treasures.
Papa

Professor Brunnabend shrugs his shoulders and smiles. "Your father never was one for too many words." He reaches inside his leather briefcase again and takes out a bundle of letters with folded pieces of old, torn papers tucked between. Alexa studies him closely, as he holds the bundle reverently in his hands and extends them across the table to her.

"He also instructed me to give you these before he left. I wasn't sure when, but I guess now is a good a time as any."

Alexa looks at the loosely wrapped bundle of papers and then back to the professor. "What is this?"

The professor glances one more time around the library and whispers, "What you haven't been told, and what is carefully kept from the press for good reason, is that your father is somewhat of a treasure hunter."

"You mean, the way he recovers stolen artifacts?"

The professor sways his head somewhat and grimaces. "*Stolen* is such a relative term. It seems that everything of value was stolen from someone at some time in history."

"Depends if they took it from the living or dead."

"Mostly the dead…"

Alexa looks directly at the professor. "Are you saying that he's a grave robber?"

"Not exactly, but that does sometimes happen."

"So, he is not the wonderful, respected teacher that I was led to believe he was?"

The professor attempts to explain further. "He is all of that, but so much more... There is a secret society of scholars and adventurers whose mission is to recover artifacts in an attempt to secure them for private institutions and for the greater good of the public."

"Who supports the funding of these endeavors?"

"Well, that's where the gray areas lie..."

"How so?"

"The museum will often fund travel expenses for such undertakings but, more often than not, it is through wealthy benefactors of the university."

"So, they somehow get a cut?"

"Depends on the prize."

Alexa looks at the bundle of papers in her hand and then down to the empty pages of the journal on the table. "And what does he want me to do with this?"

"Your father knew this trip would be during a time of conflict and danger. He spent half his life in libraries and the other on foreign soil looking for some truth to his research." The professor gestures to the bundle of paper she holds. "What you have there in your hand is what you might call his 'bucket list' of lost treasures. They are the some of the great unknowns that he would someday like to pursue."

"In the decades between visits to his family?"

The professor lowers his gaze downward, mournfully. "I believe he passed these records along to me, to give to you, as an offering of peace." He looks up at her and candid. "Knowing that you have similar interests in the historic significance of artifacts compelled him to bestow upon you his own highly-kept secrets."

"I don't want to be anything like him really."

"Do with them what you will. Hide them, if you must. Sometimes, you can't help but be who you are."

Alexa looks down at the bundled collection of papers and leather journal. She stacks them together and looks to her trusted mentor. "Thank you, Professor."

"It's the least I can do for a friend and his daughter." He nods his head, closes the flap of his briefcase, pushes his chair back and stands. The two stare at one another until Professor Brunnabend clears his throat and taps a finger on the table top. "Will I be seeing you in class this Friday?"

Alexa holds the journal and tucks the bundle of letters into her shoulder bag. She stands up from the table and a beam of sunlight from the high, gothic windows casts a luminescent light upon her. "I have three more years of university, so I suppose you'll be seeing a lot more of me yet."

Note from Author

It has been a few years since I had to pre-sell hundreds of copies of this adventure story to earn the book publishing contract. As a good friend once stated, "pre-selling a book that isn't printed yet is like trying to sell an empty box of donuts."

Well, let me tell you, it's much harder than that!

Once I hit the pre-sale goal, this book almost didn't happen. I submitted my finished manuscript with dozens of illustrations by artist, Al P. Bringas, and the reply I received was, "Sorry, but you can't have illustrations in your book." After a year-long marketing campaign to everyone I knew, I didn't have the heart to quit the publishing contract or tell my artist friend that his work was in vain. I pressed on, stating my case, explaining my experience with my New York publisher and my other western novels, until finally, they relented.

Although the publisher did a fine job of putting the book together, I saw many details that could use improving. So with this second edition of *Wings of the Pirate*, with its fresh edit, new layout of illustrations and added bonus story at the end, I guess this would be what the artist community refers to as the *Author's Cut*. Thank you to all the supporters who helped bring this story to life on the first time around so it could evolve into this new and improved edition.

Eric H. Heisner

January 10th, 2020

If you enjoyed **Wings of the Pirate**, read other stories by *Eric H. Heisner*

www.leandogproductions.com

Eric H. Heisner is an award-winning writer, actor and filmmaker. He is the author of several Western and Adventure novels: *Along to Presidio, West to Bravo, T. H. Elkman, Africa Tusk,* and the *Conch Republic* series. He can be contacted at his website:

www.leandogproductions.com

Al P. Bringas is a cowboy artist, actor and horse lover. He has done illustrations for novels including: *West to Bravo, T. H. Elkman* and *Seven Fingers a' Brazos*. He lives in Pasadena, California.

Made in the USA
Monee, IL
05 February 2021